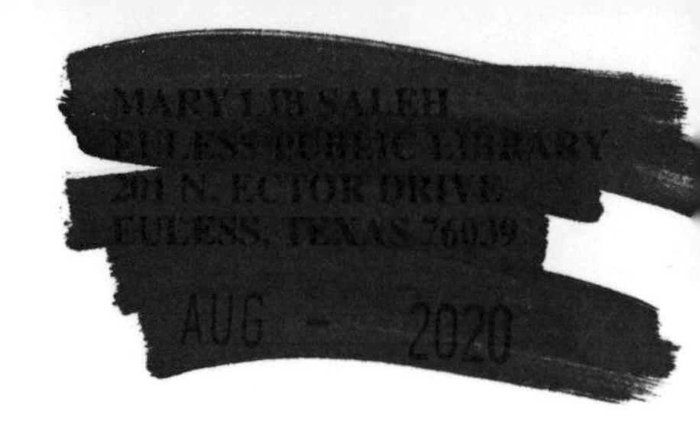
MARY LIB SALEH
EULESS PUBLIC LIBRARY
201 N. ECTOR DRIVE
EULESS, TEXAS 76039
AUG - 2020

10672243

SHIVERS!
The Pirate Who's More
Terrified than Ever

BY ANNABETH BONDOR-STONE

AND CONNOR WHITE

The Pirate Who's More Terrified than Ever

ILLUSTRATED BY
ANTHONY HOLDEN

BASED ON A REALLY FUNNY IDEA BY
HARRISON BLANZ, AGE 9

HARPER
An Imprint of HarperCollins*Publishers*

Shivers!: The Pirate Who's More Terrified than Ever
 For information address HarperCollins Children's Books, a division of HarperCollins Publishers,
195 Broadway, New York, NY 10007.
www.harpercollinschildrens.com

Library of Congress Control Number: 2019909720
ISBN 978-0-06-231393-5

Typography by Erica De Chavez
20 21 22 23 24 PC/LSCH 10 9 8 7 6 5 4 3 2 1
❖
First Edition

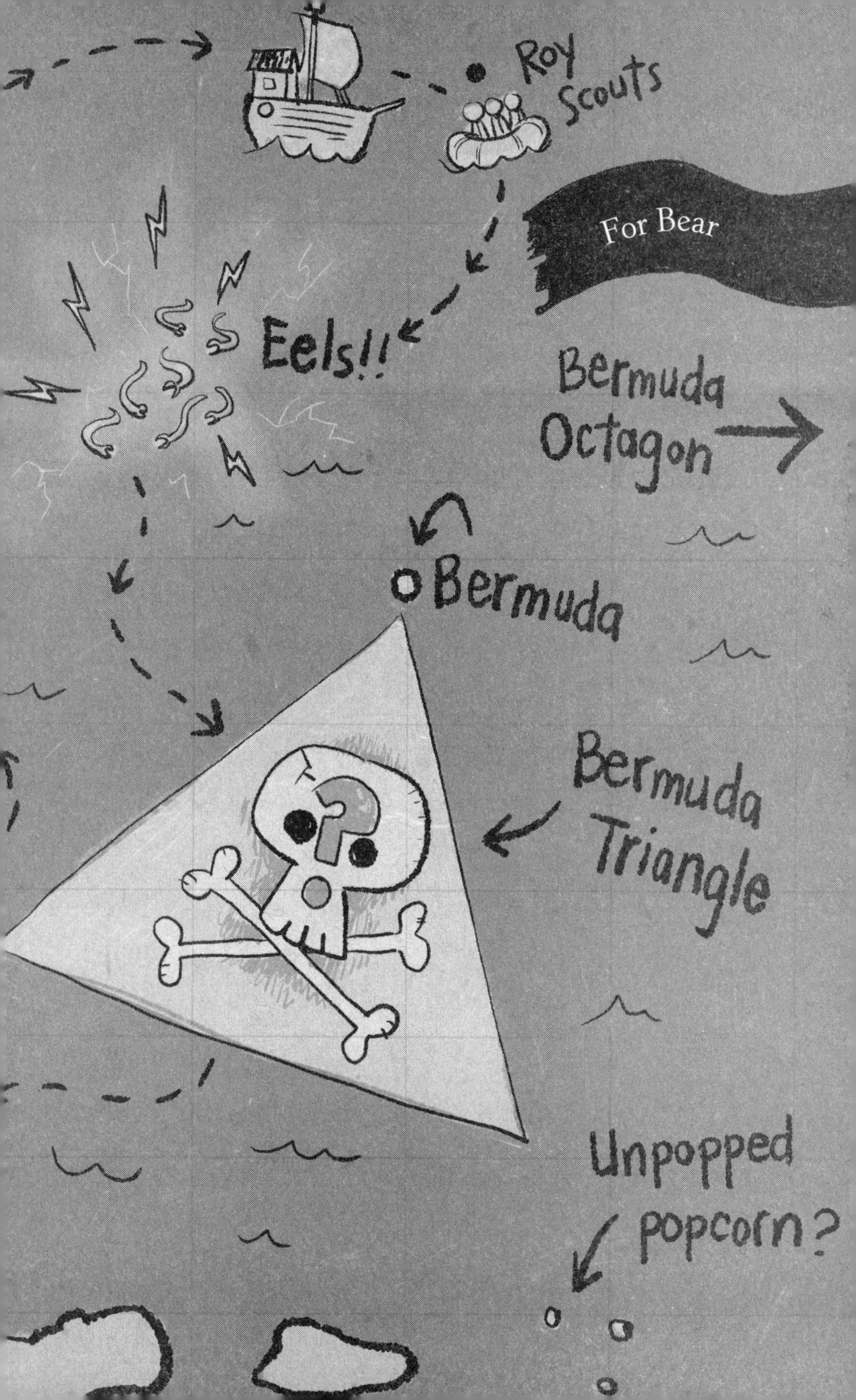

Roy Scouts

For Bear

Eels!!

Bermuda Octagon

Bermuda

Bermuda Triangle

Unpopped popcorn?

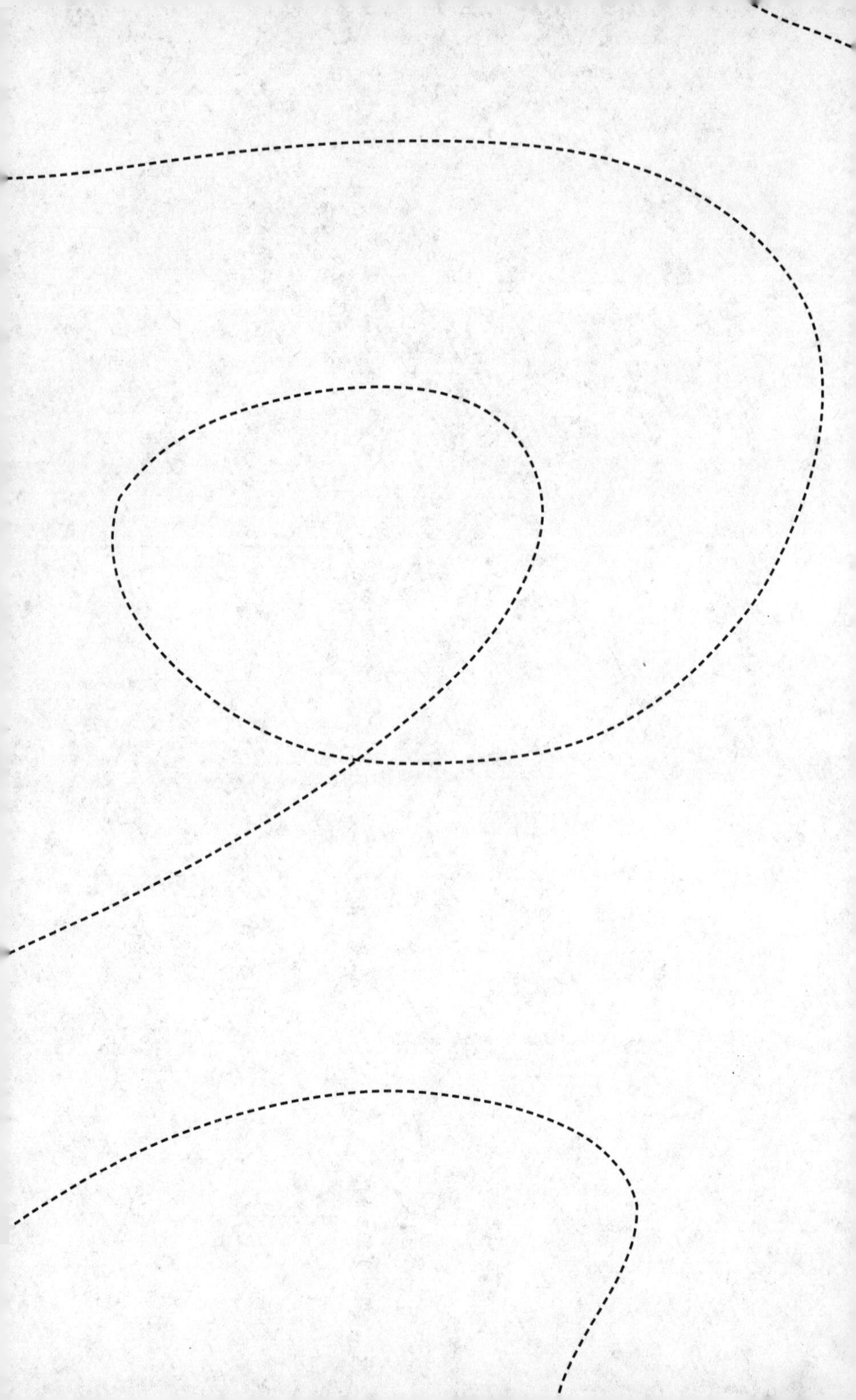

CHAPTER ONE

SNAP!

Shivers the Pirate secured the goggles to his head. The downpour had already begun. He zipped up his wet suit so his entire body was covered. Then he put on a pair of bright-yellow dish-washing gloves and wrapped rubber bands around his wrists so not a single water droplet would seep in.

"In an emergency like this, it's always good to have extra protection on hand . . . and on foot!" he declared. He swapped out his usual bunny slippers for a pair of bunny flippers. As he took a squeaky step forward, fear rattled him like a tambourine. He knew what he had to do, but he really wished he had to *don't.*

Shivers's first mate, Albee, was supervising in his fishbowl just a few feet away. Albee knew this could only end in disaster, but as a fish, there's only so much you can do. His only hope was that Shivers didn't try to use him as a flotation device.

Shivers turned to Albee and grimaced. "If I don't make it, just remember this: your fish flakes are in the cabinet. Don't eat too many at once. And never leave the stove on. In fact, don't even go near the stove." He stared straight into Albee's big, fishy eyeballs. "Use the microwave instead!"

Shivers grabbed his snorkel, crammed it into his mouth, and leaped across the great divide. Sheets of rain pelted his goggles, blurring his sight. His sopping-wet hair matted to his face. The rush of water was so strong it even seeped through his bunny flippers and tickled his toes. This was going worse than expected.

The water slapped violently against the ground.

He stuck his fingers in his ears to protect against the sound, but also to make sure the water didn't wiggle its way into his head–Shivers had always been deathly afraid of getting brainwashed.

Heavy droplets battered his scrawny legs, making him weak in the knees. Pressure swelled inside him like a balloon, until the only thing he could do was burst. He spat out the snorkel and screamed.

"AAAAAGGGHHH!!!"

But as soon as the scream started, it was snuffed out by a wave of water that funneled through Shivers's wide-open mouth. He coughed and stumbled, his flippers slipping underneath him. Shivers came crashing down with a splash as the rain pelted him harder than ever before.

"I'm drowning!" he wailed, thrashing left and splashing right.

"Pull yourself together!" Albee said, shaking his head–but because he's a fish, he was really shaking his whole body.

Then, through the misty rain, Shivers spotted his only hope for survival.

He flipped onto his belly and stretched out his arm until his fingers touched a cold, metal lever. With his last ounce of strength, he gripped it as tightly as he could and pulled.

The water stopped.

Shivers hoisted himself out of the bathtub and bellowed, "I HATE TAKING SHOWERS!"

He threw on a fresh pair of pantaloons, his velvet pirate coat, and his feathered pirate cap. He stuffed his feet into his bunny slippers and picked up Albee's fishbowl. He stumbled down the hallway and collapsed on the kitchen floor in a heap.

"That was worse than I could *ever* have imagined," he cried.

"Well, you sure smell a whole lot better!" Standing above Shivers was his best friend, Margo Clomps'n'Stomps. She stared down at him with her big green eyes, her hands on her hips. As usual, she had a backpack on her back, a ponytail on her head, and a smile as wide as a mile.

"Why did you make me do that?" Shivers groaned.

"Shivers, yesterday for your birthday, you ate six gallons of ice cream and a whole ham! You were covered in so much sugar and ham juice you smelled like a pig dipped in Pixy Stix!"

Shivers sighed. Margo had a point. Sleeping in ham juice had been unpleasant. He dragged himself up from the floor and narrowed his eyes at her. "Fine. But I'm never taking a shower again!"

Margo laughed and shook her head.

Shivers opened his refrigerator. Now that the worst part of the day was surely over, he could eat some breakfast in peace. He mixed a banana and some pudding together in a big bowl. Banana pudding was his favorite new food. It was so soft, he almost wanted to lay his head down in it and fall asleep–but then he'd have to take another shower. So instead, he plunged in his spoon and took a bite.

"Mmm . . . mushy." He grinned.

Margo sat down at the table across from him. That's when he saw the crackling flame of adventure flare in her eyes. "Oh no." Shivers waggled his finger. "I know what you're thinking, and it's got my stomach sinking. I'm going to tell you the same thing I told my family: I'm *not* going on any adventures today!"

Margo looked out the porthole and noticed that Shivers's parents' ship, the *Plunderer*, wasn't bobbing out at sea as usual. "Where did your family go?"

"Beats me! They left on a pirate mission early this morning. They said it was guaranteed to make me seasick, so I politely declined. Actually,

I screamed and hid under my covers. I'm sure they'll be back by sunset as usual, and until then, I'm staying right here."

"Come on, Shivers!" Margo slapped her palms on the table. "You can't just sit there eating pudding all day!"

"Wanna bet?" Shivers said, cramming another spoonful in his mouth.

Margo pointed out the porthole at the open ocean. "But there's a whole world of excitement out there just waiting for us!"

"Maybe it's waiting for someone else," Shivers tried. "Hey, I've got an idea–let's play hide-and-seek! You go seek out adventure, and I'll hide here under this table. Just make sure to be back by sunset. I need someone to help me turn on my night-lights."

"But we're on a pirate ship! Let's set sail! Hit the high seas!" Margo was always itching for an exciting quest.

Shivers held up his hand. "First of all, I never

hit anything. What if it hits back? Secondly, this pirate ship is designed specifically to *not* go on adventures. It's supposed to be safe, secure, and most importantly, extremely cozy. It's called the *Groundhog*, remember? And that's where it's going to stay: on the *ground*. Right here in the middle of New Jersey Beach, the safest place in the entire–AAAAAGGHHHH!!!"

At that moment, a heavy metal hook smashed through the porthole and landed on Shivers's kitchen floor. It was attached to a thick mossy rope.

"MARGO!" Shivers screamed, leaping under the table. "What's going on?!"

"Only one way to find out," she said, grabbing his hand.

They ran outside to the deck and saw something so terrifying that even the pudding in Shivers's belly panicked.

CHAPTER TWO

SHIVERS AND MARGO STOOD wide-eyed at the edge of the *Groundhog*. The mossy rope connected to the hook was tied to the most terrifying ship Shivers had ever seen. It floated in the Eastern Seas just a few yards from the sandy beach. It was so big that it cast a shadow over the entire *Groundhog*. It was coated in rotting seaweed and smelled like a fish graveyard. It rocked back and forth with an eerie creak. High on the mast was a flag with an iron lock painted on it.

Standing on the deck was a hideous man. He had a thick, mossy beard, an eye patch over one eye, and an ear patch over one ear. He wore a bloodred pirate coat so long that it brushed the floor. He had a chain of rusty keys around his neck.

"Ahoy, scoundrels!" the man shouted. "I'm Captain Crook!"

"Because you're a crook?" Shivers squeaked, hopping back and forth in terror.

"No!" Captain Crook held up his hand and wiggled his twisted, knotty fingers. "Because I have crooked fingers. That I use for stealing things. Because I'm a crook!" He laughed.

Margo stepped forward. "I'm Margo! And this is Shivers the Pirate!"

"Well, well, well . . ." Captain Crook tightrope-walked across the rope and leaped onto the

Groundhog's deck. He strolled over to Shivers, then leaned in so close that Shivers could smell his stale squid breath. "I've got one thing to say to you . . ."

Shivers was frozen in fear. For a moment, no one said anything.

Then Captain Crook bellowed, "You're welcome!" He clapped Shivers on the back and grinned, revealing a mouthful of yellow teeth that looked like broken glass.

"Huh?" Shivers, Margo, and Albee all said at the exact same time.

"We saw you were stuck on land, so now we're going to tow you out to sea. It was my first mate's idea." He turned back and shouted, "Spitball!"

A dingy-looking woman popped up from Captain Crook's deck. She had hair so wild and wiry it looked like she had stuck her finger in an electrical socket. She scurried across the rope and onto the *Groundhog*. "I've got one thing to say–"

"I already said 'you're welcome,'" said Captain Crook.

"Oh! In that case, pleasure to meet ye." Spitball grinned, and Shivers could see that she was missing her two front teeth. "Ye must be looking forward to being rescued from this awful beach."

Shivers pointed to the shore. "Actually, the beach is–"

"A horrible place!" Captain Crook interrupted. "We know. We hate it, too." Before Shivers could begin to explain all the wonders of the beach–the soft sand, the ice-cream shop, the sunbathing, which was the only kind of bathing that *didn't* involve water–Captain Crook continued, "I come to you with an offer. As I said, I'm a crook. I takes what I wants and I wants a whole lot. But I can't do it alone. I'm assembling a pirate crew. A fearsome pirate crew. A *deadly* pirate crew."

"A particularly smelly pirate crew!" Spitball added, scratching her armpit.

Shivers looked over at Captain Crook's ship. Sure enough, he saw dozens of fearsome figures lurking on the deck.

"This crew is going to break *all* the rules! I've got big, big plans!" Captain Crook raised his

eyebrow. "And I'm looking for new members."

"Me? Join a terrifying pirate crew?" Shivers squeaked.

"Why not?" Captain Crook strode across the deck and into the kitchen. Shivers and Margo followed behind him. He stomped his black boot on the floor. "You've got a sturdy ship." He pointed at Margo. "You've got a first mate." He gestured to the kitchen table. "Why, you've even got a giant bowl of guts right here!"

"Guts?!" Shivers gagged. "That's pudding!"

Slowly, Captain Crook turned to Shivers, squinting his eye. "Pudding?" he asked.

"Banana pudding," said Shivers. "Want some?"

"Pirates don't eat pudding," Captain Crook sputtered.

"We eat cod cake and dead coral!" Spitball added.

"Gross!" said Shivers. "Just thinking about that is making me queasy. He gripped his stomach. "I think I'm getting *C*-sick."

"A pirate who gets seasick?" Captain Crook curled up his lip like a caterpillar doing crunches.

"Seasick, *C*-sick, see-sick . . . It's all awful to me," Shivers explained. "That's why I live on land."

"Live on land?!" Captain Crook shouted. He paced furiously around the kitchen. "You *live* on *land*?"

"Well, sure!" said Shivers.

Captain Crook threw his hands in the air. "I can't believe my ear!" He glared at Shivers with his one bloodshot eye. "You're not a real pirate at all. You're just a landlubber in funny pants!" He nodded at Spitball and commanded, "Spit 'em up!"

With a gleeful look in her eye, Spitball stood at attention, leaned her head back, then hocked a barrage of slimy spit-shots through the gap in her front teeth. Shivers and Margo covered their heads and hit the deck as the glistening wads of saliva whizzed past them. They shattered Shivers's teacups, pinged off his pie tins, and even mashed the Potato button on his microwave.

Then, Spitball did something that took everyone by surprise, even Captain Crook. She grabbed Albee's fishbowl and ran down the hall, cackling like a crazy person.

"Albee!" Shivers screamed, his eyes popping with panic.

He and Margo leaped up and ran after Spitball. They caught up to her just in time to see her pour Albee from his fishbowl into the toilet bowl.

"NO!" Shivers and Margo shouted.

But it was too late. Spitball grabbed the handle and flushed.

SHIVERS WAS O-FISH-IALLY PANICKED. After flushing Albee, Spitball and Captain Crook ran back to their ship, laughing and high-fiving each other. But Shivers found nothing funny about this potty humor.

"Hold on, Albee!" Shivers shouted. Then he turned to Margo. "What am I saying?! He can't hold on to anything with those fins!" There was only one thing to do. "I'm coming for you, buddy!" Shivers cried. He kicked off his bunny slippers and jumped into the toilet. But as soon as his toes touched the water he shrieked, "I'm drowning! Help!" and Margo had to pull him

back out. He collapsed on the bathroom floor . . . for the second time that day. "I failed my first mate!" he cried. Then he had an idea. "Margo, you know how to swim! Get in there!"

"Shivers, neither of us is going to fit down the toilet," Margo insisted.

Shivers lifted himself to his knees and looked at Margo with tears in his eyes. "You can at least *try*!"

"I've got a better idea. Follow me!"

Margo ran out of the ship and onto the beach. She headed toward town as fast as she could. Shivers struggled to keep up, sweating like a soda can left out in the sun. They sprinted past the soft serve at the ice-cream shop and the hard serves at the volleyball nets. They leaped over lines of sand-caked sunbathers until they finally reached the sidewalks of New Jersey.

Margo scanned the street until she spotted what she was looking for. Just up the road, next to a construction site, was an entrance to the sewer.

"Come on! We've got to get into that manhole!" Margo shouted, sensing adventure on the horizon–or rather, deep inside the sewer.

"Manhole?" Shivers said nervously. "Isn't there a pirate hole somewhere?"

But Margo was already busy trying to pry the heavy metal cover off the hole. "Shivers, help!" she groaned.

"This must have been for one large, circular man," said Shivers, getting on his knees to lift with her.

They yanked; they pried; they pulled; but even with all of Margo's might and all of Shivers's fright, they couldn't get the cover to budge.

Shivers banged on the top of the manhole as hard as he could in sheer desperation. "Hello?! Albee?! If you're down there, let us in! We're trying to save you!" His face crumpled in agony. "Why doesn't this thing have a doorbell?"

"Don't worry, Shivers. We'll get in that sewer somehow," she said, searching frantically for a solution. Then she pointed to a section of the block that was surrounded by orange cones. "Look! The construction site!"

"How is that going to help?" Shivers whined.

Margo suggested, "Maybe we could borrow a hammer–"

"For what?! I already ate all the ham!"

Margo sighed. "Well, there's a forklift–"

"Margo! Get your head in the game! Do you see any forks around here?" Shivers pulled at his hair, deep in thought. "What we *really* need is a car with a giant arm and a long dangling hook that can lift this manhole cover right out of the ground. Preferably painted yellow. If only such a thing existed!"

Margo tapped Shivers on the shoulder. "You mean like *that*?" she gestured toward a giant yellow crane in the middle of the construction site.

"Well, I'd prefer if it were *more* yellow. . . ." said Shivers.

They dashed off toward the construction site, and suddenly Shivers was seized with fear. He saw a sign that, like most signs, he took as a bad sign.

"That says 'Hard Hats Only'! And I have the softest hat of all," he said, touching his velvet pirate hat.

Margo grabbed Shivers's arm and pulled him

behind a big orange barrel. "Forget about the hats! We've got bigger fish to fry!"

"You're lucky Albee didn't hear you say that," Shivers said.

Margo peeked out from behind the barrel and saw three construction workers sitting on the curb eating their lunch. "Okay," she whispered, "I'm going to go borrow that crane. And you . . . are on distraction duty!" she shoved Shivers toward the workers. By the time he turned around to argue, she had already scampered away, her big green backpack bouncing behind her.

Shivers approached the workers, who all wore bright-orange vests and yellow hats. One guy had on mirrored sunglasses. The one sitting in the middle had a tattoo on her arm that said EAT MY SAWDUST. And the third was wearing a tool belt that was *not* doing a good job of keeping his pants up.

The guy in the sunglasses was about to take a

bite of his sandwich when he spotted Shivers and shouted, "Hey, kid! You can't be in here. Construction workers only."

"I . . ." Shivers thought fast. "I am a construction worker! *Lunch* construction," he said, taking another step toward them. "And I'm sorry to inform you that these lunches are not up to code."

The workers looked at him suspiciously.

"What have you got there?" Shivers asked, pointing at the lunch boxes.

"Peanut butter and jelly with a side of chips," said the man in sunglasses.

"A chicken sandwich with fries, same as every day." The tattooed woman shrugged.

"Just a salad," the guy with the tool belt said sadly. "I'm watching my weight."

"Good idea. You never know when it might sneak up on you." Shivers shuddered and then pressed on. "People, you've got it all wrong! We're going to need a major renovation here. But first, I'm going to need to borrow a hard hat. If there's one thing I know about lunch, it's that things can get messy."

The woman with the tattoo handed over her yellow hat. Shivers put the hard hat on top of his soft hat, grabbed the three lunch boxes, and got to work. He mixed and matched ingredients, his hands flying between the meals so fast that the workers couldn't help but look on in amazement. He crisscrossed the crusts, retossed the salad, and unjammed the jelly from its peanut-buttery

partner. Finally, he presented the workers with their new and improved meals.

He turned to the man with the tool belt. "Your salad was looking a little soggy, so I added in chips for extra crunch!"

"Thank you!" The man grinned. "What a salty surprise!"

Then, Shivers handed a lunch box to the man in sunglasses. "For you, peanut butter–battered chicken. In some parts of the world, this is considered a delicacy." He leaned in and whispered, like he was sharing a secret, "And in others, they haven't even *heard* of it."

"Ooh! How exotic!" the worker replied with excitement.

"And finally, my greatest creation," Shivers said, strolling over to the tattooed woman. "Introducing . . . jelly fries!"

"Oh," the woman said with much less enthusiasm. But when she tried a french fry dipped in grape jelly, she jumped to her feet and shouted, "It's brilliant! BRILLIANT!"

Shivers blushed. "I'm glad you like it. As I always say, once it's in your belly, it's *all* jelly!"

The three workers dug into their meals with gusto, throwing their heads back in delight with every bite. They were so busy enjoying their new and improved lunches that they didn't even notice the ten-year-old girl stealing–or, rather, borrowing–the giant crane right behind them.

Margo had never operated a crane before, but she had spent a lot of time (and money) playing the claw game at the arcade, so she caught on pretty quickly. She looped the hook into the manhole cover and lifted it clean off. Then she hopped out of the crane and gave Shivers a big thumbs-up.

Shivers said, "Well, folks, I wish I could stay and chat. But I don't have the right hat." He took off the hard hat and returned it to the tattooed woman. Then he turned to go.

"Wait!" said the man with the tool belt. "Who are you?"

Shivers looked back and squinted in the sun-light. "I'm just a kid looking for a fish."

He ran to the edge of the manhole, where Margo was waiting. They linked their arms, plugged their noses, and dove in.

CHAPTER FOUR

SHIVERS AND MARGO LANDED in the sewer sludge with a SKLURSH–which is kind of like a splash, but much more disgusting. They were instantly swept up in a gurgling current of grime and slime.

Shivers flailed around in the soggy darkness, trying to grab hold of Margo as they slid through the sewer. "Why didn't you tell me there weren't any lights down here?!" he shrieked.

"Shivers, trust me: sometimes it's better to be in the dark," Margo shouted back.

As they twisted around a corner, their eyes began to adjust to the dim light streaming in through the street grates above them. Now, Shivers saw what they were sliding in. It was a slug-green swirl of mold and curdled milk, served with a side of stinky slush. Shivers and Margo spotted a faint glimmer of a blowfish tail flapping up ahead.

"Albee!!!" they called out, their voices echoing off the sewer walls.

But Albee was being funneled through the tunnel just as fast as Shivers and Margo were. Suddenly, he slipped out of sight. Shivers squinted to see where Albee had gone and realized they were sliding straight toward a sheer drop-off. Judging from the sound of the sludge splashing below, it was going to be a big drop.

"AAAAAGH!" Shivers screamed. He grabbed Margo and swung her in front of him. "Margo, you're really the leader of this mission. You get in front!" he said, grabbing her shoulders.

Shivers and Margo flew with the force of a thousand flushes toward the drop-off. They spotted a sign right at the edge that said, WELCOME TO UNDERNEATH DOWNTOWN NEW JERSEY—WHERE GARBAGE GOES TO DIE!

"Whoa, cool!" Margo said. "I bet this is one of those places only the locals know about!"

Shivers tried to wrap himself up in her backpack straps and wailed, "I DON'T WANT TO BE DEAD GARBAGE!"

It was a reasonable request, but the current was only moving one way. Shivers searched desperately for something to

hold on to. He dragged his hands through the muck until he finally found a net. But it was a hairnet . . . made of hair. He screamed and tossed it aside.

Now, they were just inches away from the drop. In one last attempt, Shivers plunged his arms deep into the sludge. He sifted through the grit and grime and then, just in time, his fingers wrapped around a thick rope.

"Margo! We're saved!" he fear-cheered.

But when he yanked the rope out of the sludge, he saw that it was attached to a brown, bulbous body with a furry head . . . And that it wasn't a rope at all, but the tail of a snarling sewer rat.

Dread shot from the top of Shivers's head to the tips of his slippers. He shrieked so loudly that he woke up the *rest* of the sewer rats, who popped their heads up and glowered at Shivers with cranky red eyes.

"AAAAAAAGH!" he wailed,

flinging the rat into the darkness and flailing his hands in the air as he came to the drop-off.

"Great idea!" Margo said. "Hands up for the big drop!"

And with that, they sailed over the edge and fell through the air until the big drop turned into the big plop as they landed in the soupy sewer water below.

The current picked them up again, and now they were in an even larger tunnel. The damp, mossy walls were dotted with big holes, and sunlight streamed down from the street above.

Margo looked up. "We're right under Main Street!"

"The only thing I'm under is extreme stress!" Shivers moaned, still sliding behind her.

"If my coordinates are right, we should be directly underneath the Candy Bar and Grill," Margo said.

It turned out her coordinates *were* right, and all the trash from the candy store came tumbling through the hole above their heads.

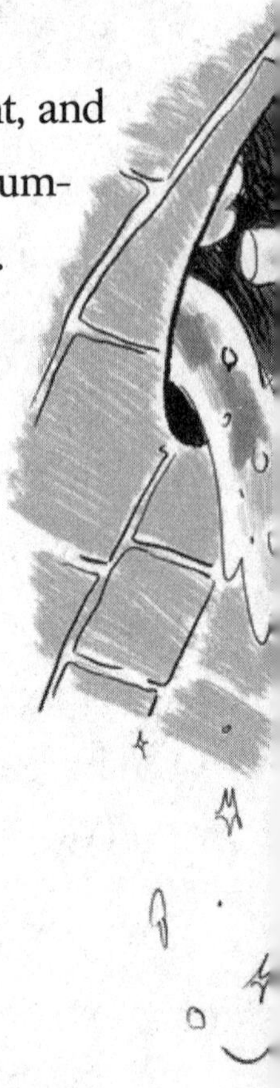

"Incoming!" Shivers shouted, shoving Margo firmly in front of him.

She was hit with a barrage of stale-but-still-soft marshmallows. Seconds later, Shivers was pelted with Pop Rocks that exploded around him as they hit the water.

"AAGGH! A SNACK ATTACK!" he screamed.

"Don't worry," Margo shouted as the current continued to carry them. "We're coming up on the flower shop! What could go wrong?"

Just then, Dolores, the florist from the Petal Peddler, poured a sackful of surplus roses into the sewer.

The petals fluttered down and gently brushed Margo's face. "Mm, smells nice!" she said, smiling.

Then, the thorns shot straight at Shivers, poking him all over.

"Aggh! I don't want my ears pierced!" he wailed.

"That's it! I'm getting in front!"

Shivers scrambled past Margo just as they were rushed beneath the craft store. As it turned out, Make Your Own Junk was going out of business, so they were dumping all their junk from the store into the sewer. All at once, Shivers was drenched in a shower of glue, feathers, and beads that made him look like a bedazzled chicken. Margo got lightly dusted with glitter.

They reached the end of the sewer and got spit out into a pool of shallow, murky seawater. They looked around and realized they were right under a New Jersey pier. Huge wooden pillars towered above them, supporting a bustling boardwalk that stretched far out into the ocean. They could hear the clatter of rushing roller coasters above them. The thick smell of smoked meats and fried cheese filled their noses.

"Albee?! Where are you?!" Shivers squawked, flapping around frantically in the water.

An old man and woman leaned over the pier's edge and saw Shivers.

“Look, darling! It’s one of New Jersey’s famous sewer chickens!” the man said, snapping a picture.

Shivers and Margo waded through the salty slosh, searching desperately for any sign of Albee.

“We’ll never find him!” Shivers wailed. “He could be anywhere in this giant salt bucket!”

“I’m right here!” Albee called out from the open ocean ahead. But as usual, no one could hear him.

Shivers fell to his knees and sobbed. "Everyone always told me there are other fish in the sea, but I want *my* fish!"

"I'M RIGHT HERE!" Albee shouted at the top of his gills. He mustered all his strength and puffed up to his full blowfish size.

"There he is!" Margo cheered. Without giving it a second thought, she dove into the water and swam with all her might until she reached Albee. She grabbed a spare sandwich bag from her backpack and scooped Albee up inside, then swam back to shore.

She handed Albee back to Shivers, who gave the sandwich bag a big hug.

"We'll never let you out of our sight again," he promised.

Margo noticed that Shivers had managed to shake off some of the feathers but was still almost entirely crusted in crud. "You're going to have to take another shower," she warned him.

"NEVER!" Shivers shouted. "I've almost drowned six times today, and I haven't even had my mid-morning nap! Come on, Albee, let's go home."

They turned to head toward the sand, but then Margo saw something that stopped her in her tracks. Floating near the sewer entrance was a green glass bottle with a piece of paper inside.

"A message in a bottle!" she gasped. Her green eyes sparkled–and not just because she was still covered in glitter. "I've always wanted to find one of these! We've got to read what's inside!"

"Why?" Shivers shrugged. "We already know what it's going to say."

Margo scooped the bottle out of the water. "What do you mean?"

Shivers shook his head and sighed, "Margo, it's a message in a bottle. It's obviously going to say 'Help! Let me out of this bottle!'"

Shivers didn't really understand what a message in a bottle was.

Margo plopped down on the sandy beach, popped the cork, and read the message. By the time she reached the end, the excitement on her face had slipped away, and a darkness had fallen over her eyes.

Shivers sat down next to her and clutched Albee's bag nervously. "What's wrong?" he asked.

Margo showed him the paper. It was drenched in seawater and the ink had run, but Shivers could still make out the message:

To Whom It May Concern
(and it concerns everybody),
Captain Crook is going to
attack New Jersey!
No beachgoer or sunbather is
safe! Everyone is in danger!
The key to stopping him is
inside the treasure chest in
the Bermuda Triangle.
If ye have found this
message, congratulations! Yer
still alive! Now HELP!
Signed,

But the paper was too soggy to see the signature.

CHAPTER FIVE

SHIVERS WAS HORRIFIED. HIS mouth dropped to the ground in shock and stayed for so long that a sand crab almost moved in. "Captain Crook is going to attack New Jersey?!"

"That's what the message says," Margo said through gritted teeth. She was furious that anyone, pirate or otherwise, was threatening her town.

Shivers wasn't furious; he *was* fear-ious. "He can't do that! Pirates never attack people on land. It's the number-one rule of the Pirate Code!"

"The Pirate *what*?" Margo asked.

"The Pirate Code! The rules that all pirates have followed for hundreds of years!"

"Pirates always have to follow these rules?" Margo asked.

"Always," Shivers insisted. "Without the Pirate Code, the sea would be chaos! Pirates would just be a bunch of hideous heathens doing whatever they wanted! Have you ever seen a pirate talk back to a whale?"

"No . . ." said Margo.

"Of course not! Because that's rule number eighteen!" Shivers began to pace back and forth, rattling off the rules of the Pirate Code. "Rule number six: First the skull, then the crossbones. Number eleven: Never ride a seahorse. Number forty-two: *Always* sail away from the puke." He turned to Margo with wide eyes. "And do you ever wonder why I'm always screaming so loudly?"

Margo cocked her head. "Because you're afraid of everything?"

"Well, yes . . . But also because of rule number three." Shivers shouted, "ALWAYS USE YOUR OUTSIDE VOICE!" He stopped in his tracks and threw his hands in the air. "But the most important rule is rule number one: Pirates never attack people on land."

Margo picked up the message. "Well, it looks like Captain Crook and his whole gruesome crew are going to break the Pirate Code. And there's only one thing we can do about it–"

"Return this letter to where it came from!" Shivers snatched the paper from her. "It was much less scary when it was a message *in* a bottle than when it was a message *out* of a bottle." He rolled up the mushy paper. "Let's toss it back into the ocean, head home, and figure out the snack of the day!" He tried to stuff the paper into the bottle, but Margo yanked it back.

"Shivers, you can't just fix something by throwing it in the water."

Shivers shook his head. "That's what *I* said when you made me take a shower!"

"We've got to do something about this!" said Margo.

Just then, they heard the wail of sirens as a squad of police cars zipped down the street.

"Margo, look! Help is on the way!" Shivers grabbed Albee's bag and sprinted after the police cars. Margo followed close behind. Her dad, Police Chief Clomps'n'Stomps, would know what to do.

Margo and Shivers reached the edge of the beach and saw the police squad gathered in front of old Mrs. Sternbean's house. Their black-and-white cars were parked haphazardly along

the sidewalk. Police Chief Clomps'n'Stomps was barking orders at the whole squad. He was standing next to Mrs. Sternbean; her tiny wrinkled head poked out of a huge knit sweater.

"Okay, people, get in position!" Clomps shouted. "Code red!"

Shivers and Margo ran onto the lawn.

"Margo!" Clomps said, his eyes lighting up. "And . . . Shivers," he added, his eyes dimming down. "What are you doing here? It's Sunday. Aren't you supposed to be hiding from the sun?"

"Normally, yes." Shivers gasped, trying to catch his breath from all the running. "But we've got a big problem!"

Clomps grunted. "I know we do. I'm taking care of it right now." He held up a big white megaphone and announced, "I don't know how Cuddles the kitten got stuck in that tree, but we're not leaving until we get him down!"

"YES, SIR!" the squad shouted back.

That's when Shivers and Margo noticed the fluffy white cat perched on the highest branch of Mrs. Sternbean's maple tree. The police officers leaned a large metal ladder against the tree and started climbing.

"We have a much bigger problem than this!" said Shivers.

"There is no bigger problem than this," Mrs. Sternbean wailed. "Except for how many hairballs I have in my house. But that's *my* problem."

Margo tugged on Clomps's sleeve. "Dad, we found a message–"

"The only message I want to hear right now is that Cuddles is safely on the ground! The rest will have to wait!" said Clomps.

Margo sighed. She knew that when her dad was on the job, nothing could stop him. The only way to get his attention was to get the cat out of the tree first.

The officers scrambled from branch to branch,

calling "Here, kitty, kitty!" But Cuddles, like most cats, only had one trick–ignoring people.

Margo realized that the only way to catch this cat was to make it come to them. She turned to Mrs. Sternbean. "What are Cuddles's favorite things?"

Mrs. Sternbean's face lit up. "Well, he likes batting fish around."

"Not going to happen!" said Albee.

Mrs. Sternbean continued, "All his favorite toys are bouncy, squeaky, and covered in feathers."

Margo looked over at Shivers. He was bouncing nervously in his bunny slippers and letting out high-pitched squeaks, the feather on his pirate hat flapping in the wind. It dawned on her, for the first time since she'd known him, that Shivers was basically a giant cat toy. She grabbed her dad's megaphone and announced, "Send in the pirate!"

And with that, Shivers was grabbed by the

long arm of the law–in fact it was several long arms–which lifted him up and flung him into the tree.

"AAAAAAGH!" Shivers screamed as he landed in a thicket of branches just inches away from Cuddles. Shivers turned to face the cat, and his whole being filled with dread. Sure, kittens looked cute in pictures, but up close they were cringe-inducing.

Cuddles wiggled his whiskers. Shivers leaped back and screamed, "Don't whisk me!"

Then Cuddles swatted at Shivers's hat. Shivers ducked and shouted, "Press pause on those paws!"

The more Shivers quivered, the more curious Cuddles grew. He pounced toward him. Shivers knew that even if he defeated the cat once, he would have to do it again *eight more times*! It just wasn't a fair fight! He decided to make a run for it. And then he made a stumble for it. And then he made a fall for it.

As Shivers hurtled toward the ground, Cuddles leaped out of the tree after him. Fortunately, the police squad was ready with a giant safety net. They caught Cuddles comfortably in the net just as Shivers came crashing down into Mrs. Sternbean's birdbath.

Mrs. Sternbean scooped Cuddles up in her arms and announced, "Cookies and lemonade for everyone!"

"Cookies *and* lemonade?!" one of the officers remarked.

"What a refreshing treat!" another officer shouted.

The squad stampeded into Mrs. Sternbean's house. Clomps stayed behind and helped Margo pull Shivers out of the birdbath.

Shivers was spitting and sputtering, flinging filthy bathwater everywhere. "A shower and a bath in one morning?" He groaned. "This is the worst day ever!"

Clomps looked down at Margo. She had his full attention now. "So what's the big problem?" he asked.

"We found a message in a bottle that says a pirate named Captain Crook is going to attack the people of New Jersey!" said Margo.

Clomps let out a chuckle. Margo didn't see what was so funny. "That's not going to happen." he said, patting her on the shoulder with his big meaty hand. "Pirates never attack people on land. It's the number-one rule of the Pirate Code."

"That's what *I* said." Shivers brushed a twig out of his hair.

"But what if he does?" said Margo. "The message says that the key to stopping him is in the Bermuda Triangle."

Clomps arched an eyebrow. "The Bermuda Triangle?"

"That's right," said Shivers. "The one and only!"

"*The* Bermuda Triangle?"

"Uh-huh." Shivers nodded.

"The Bermuda Triangle!" Clomps cried. "Everybody knows that the Bermuda Triangle is the most dangerous place on earth! No one who's been there has ever come back–*ever*! You'd have to be crazy to go to the Bermuda Triangle just because of some soggy note."

"But, Dad–"

Clomps held up his hand. "I'm sorry, Margo. I've got to get ready for Cheese Curd Night."

"Cheese Curd Night?" Shivers dared to ask, already feeling a little *C*-sick at the thought of it.

Clomps pulled a flyer out of his back pocket and handed it to Shivers. "That's right," Clomps said. "It's the biggest cheese-themed celebration of the year. The whole town comes out to play games, ride rides, and eat buckets and buckets of fried cheese. Last year, they ran out of cheese early, and things got . . . crazy." He shuddered. "I'm going to go round up the squad." He turned to go into Mrs. Sternbean's house, but when he saw Margo's concerned expression,

he crouched down and looked into her green eyes. “Don’t worry; everything’s going to be fine. Unless they run out of cheese again . . .” He walked into Mrs. Sternbean’s house and closed the door behind him.

Margo turned to Shivers with her hands on her hips. “Well, looks like we need a new plan.”

“Wait!” His face lit up. “Have we tried waking ourselves up and realizing this was all just a really bad dream?”

Margo pinched Shivers’s scrawny arm, and he screamed, “AAGH! It’s real life!”

"That's right. Which means we have to stop Captain Crook ourselves." She marched off with Albee in one hand and the message in a bottle in the other. "It's a long journey to the Bermuda Triangle. Let's get your ship ready."

"For what? A horrifying shipwreck?" Shivers ran after her. "You heard what your dad said. The Bermuda Triangle is the most dangerous place in the entire world! My ship will be destroyed! We'll be swallowed by the sea!"

"Shivers, we're the only ones who can save New Jersey," Margo called back. "This is my home. And it's your home, too. Look around–everything you love is here. The ice-cream stand . . . the Mop Stop . . . the pop-up popcorn shop!"

Shivers smiled dreamily. "I love it when that shop pops up."

"If we don't do something to stop Captain Crook, it might never pop up again."

"But Margo, sailing to the Bermuda Triangle

is crazy! It's crazier than crazy! It's what a crazy person would call crazy!" He stopped to think for a second. "Or is it what a crazy person would call normal? Either way, it's a terrible idea!"

"If you think that's scary, think of what will happen if we let Captain Crook attack. He'll destroy everything here, including us!" Margo looked Shivers straight in the eye. "Sure, we might sink your ship."

Shivers gasped.

"Sure, we might end up trapped in the most dangerous place on earth."

Shivers squeaked.

"And sure, we might end up buried in a squid cemetery. But we *have* to try!"

"But we're sailing into certain destruction!" Shivers squealed.

"If you want to conquer your fears, you have to face them head-on," Margo said. "I heard that from the guy at the helmet store."

Shivers wasn't sure what to say. Albee was speechless. By now, they had reached Shivers's ship. Margo led the way up to the main deck and gestured around them to the beach, the pier, and the town behind them. "This is our home. We have to fight for it." She grabbed him by the shoulders. "Are you with me?"

Shivers realized that Margo was right. He loved his town. He loved his beach. But Margo forgot the thing he loved most about New Jersey. It was where his best friend lived. He might have been filled with fear, but the choice was clear. He took a deep breath. "I can't believe I'm about to say this," he whispered. "Let's go to the Bermuda Triangle."

Margo smiled. She raced up to the captain's deck and grabbed the helm. "It's do or die!" she shouted.

"Or both . . ." said Albee. But fortunately, nobody heard him.

CHAPTER SIX

AS THE *GROUNDHOG* FLOATED out onto the open ocean, Margo realized that as sure as she was that they had to get to the Bermuda Triangle, she had no idea which way to go.

"Shivers? Do you have a map?" she called down to the main deck.

"Are you kidding me?! Have you ever tried to unfold one of those things? You need a map for the map! Not to mention a pair of protective gloves–a map is a paper cut waiting to happen."

"But I do have something else." Shivers ran inside, then came back to the captain's deck holding a globe. "I hold it when I want to feel big."

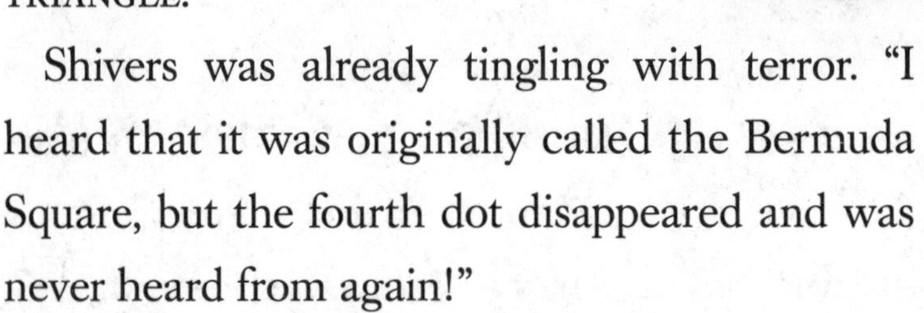

"Perfect!" Margo spun the globe around until she saw three small dots in the Southern Seas. Between them were the words BERMUDA TRIANGLE.

Shivers was already tingling with terror. "I heard that it was originally called the Bermuda Square, but the fourth dot disappeared and was never heard from again!"

Margo was too busy setting the course for the Southern Seas to pay attention. While she steered the ship over the rolling waves, Shivers and Albee went to the kitchen. Shivers gave Albee a snack of fish flakes and butter, then decided to see if banana-pudding popcorn was a tasty snack. It wasn't.

Shivers stepped out onto the deck. "Margo, you've got to try this banana-pudding popcorn! It's disgusting!"

"Um, no, thanks," Margo called down. She turned back to the helm just in time to see a bright-yellow raft full of people drift into their path. "Watch out!" Margo shouted, spinning the helm so hard to the right that it felt wrong. The ship veered to the side, narrowly missing the raft and sending Shivers tumbling over. Banana-pudding popcorn spilled everywhere.

"AAAGH!" he shouted. "I need a fresh mop!"

"Ahoy there, sailors!" a voice called out from below. Standing at the front of the raft was a tall man with a ponytail and a friendly smile. He was sporting a bright-orange life vest and had a guitar strapped to his back. "My name's Roy!" he announced. "And these are the Roy Scouts!"

Shivers and Margo peered over the railing and noticed that the raft was filled with kids who were also wearing orange life vests.

"Ahoy!" the kids said in perfect unison as they all gave thumbs-ups.

"That's a lot of thumbs," Shivers whispered to Margo.

"The *Roy Scouts*?" Margo asked.

"That's right!" Roy replied. As the scouts rowed the raft alongside the ship, he explained, "We explore the outdoors and sing catchy songs, all while putting safety first!"

Shivers's eyes lit up and he leaned over the railing. "I'm listening. . . ."

"Well, if you're *really* listening, you wouldn't lean so far over that railing! It's dangerous!" said Roy.

"You're right!" Shivers jumped back.

The kids all cheered. "He's learning already!" one of them shouted.

"Give him a safety patch!" another one urged.

Roy reached into a knapsack full of colorful

patches and flung one up to Shivers. Shivers screamed and ducked. Margo caught it and handed it to him. The badge said SAFETY along the edge and was embroidered with a picture of a man covering his head. "It looks just like me!" Shivers exclaimed. He peeled off the sticky backing and slapped it onto his velvet pirate coat. "I get a sticker just for being safe?"

"You get a patch for every achievement when you're a Roy Scout," Roy beamed. "Isn't that right?"

"WE LOVE PATCHES!" the kids yelled. All of their scout uniforms were covered in brightly colored patches.

Roy continued, "And every day after our adventures are over, we gather around the fire to tell–"

"Ghost stories?" Margo guessed.

"No!" Roy looked at Margo like she was insane. "Toast stories! We talk about our favorite kinds of toast and jam!"

"Are you kidding me?!" Shivers clutched his hat. "This guy is incredible!"

Margo could see where this was going. If she didn't act fast, Shivers would be tempted to stay here forever, and they'd never make it to the Bermuda Triangle. "Well, it was nice to meet you. We have to get going now."

"Where are you off to?" Roy asked.

"The Bermuda Triangle," said Margo. She moved to go back to the helm, but Roy signaled for the scouts to paddle faster until they drifted in front of the ship, blocking its path.

"The Bermuda Triangle? That doesn't sound very safe," said Roy.

"Thanks for the warning, but we've got to get there right away," Margo called down. "We don't have time to talk."

"But do you have time"–Roy unstrapped the guitar from his back–"to sing?"

"*Do* I?!" Shivers exclaimed. He leaped over to the grand piano on his deck and fluttered his fingers across the keys. "It just so happens that singing is one of my two specialties. The other is dancing!" He tapped out a tiny little dance. "I call that the tippy-tap!" he said.

The Roy Scouts burst into applause. Roy strummed his guitar and led the scouts in song. Shivers tried to follow along on the piano while hitting all the high notes.

Roy Scouts, Roy Scouts
We don't light fires, we don't use matches!
Roy Scouts, Roy Scouts
We only care about getting patches!

Roy Scouts, Roy Scouts
We think that danger is the worst!

Roy Scouts, Roy Scouts
After patches, safety's first!

Jump for joy,
Jump for Roy,
Scream and shout,
Roy Scoooooooouts!

Shivers held the final note longer than anyone. When the song came to an end, all the scouts were looking up at him, amazed at his angelic voice.

"Singing patches for everyone!" Roy announced. He reached into his bag and tossed patches in all directions as the scouts jumped up to catch them. Shivers rushed over to the railing to get his patch. "Over here!" he shouted, leaning all the way over with his arms outstretched.

"Shivers–" Margo warned.

But it was too late. Roy flung a round life preserver through the air, and it landed around Shiver's shoulders like he was a human ring toss.

"PULL!" Roy bellowed.

The scouts yanked on the rope that was attached to the life preserver, and Shivers tumbled down onto the raft. "AAAAAAGH!"

As soon as Shivers landed, Roy slapped a patch onto his coat that looked like the inside of a giant mouth. "That's your screaming patch," Roy said.

Margo ran to the edge of the ship. "Hey! What in the Seven Seas do you think you're doing?!"

"Saving you from yourselves!" said Roy. "You can't go to the Bermuda Triangle. It's much too dangerous!"

"That argument doesn't work on her," said Shivers, trying to wriggle free from the life preserver.

"Give me back my best friend!" Margo demanded, her green eyes sharpening like two swords.

Roy stepped to the edge of the raft. "Listen, little lady. If I let you go to the Bermuda Triangle and your ship sinks–and we all know it will–that would just break my big old heart." He turned back to the scouts. "GET HER!"

One of the bigger scouts hoisted up a heavy rope from the floor of the raft. As he swung it around his head like a lasso, Margo could see that there was a hook attached to the end. He tossed the rope up in the air and hooked it onto the ship's railing.

"Who wants a climbing patch?!" said Roy, holding a fistful of patches above his head.

"PATCHES!" the Scouts shouted with glee. They scrambled onto the rope and started climbing up toward the ship.

"Don't let them get to you, Margo!" Shivers called up to her.

Margo darted around the deck, searching for something to cut the rope before the Roy Scouts got on board, but everything on Shivers's ship was soft and cozy. Even the sharp keys on his piano were covered in plush padding. She sprinted around a corner and skidded to a stop in front of a door labeled AX ROOM.

"Don't worry! I found the Ax Room!" she shouted down to Shivers.

"Uh, Margo–"

She flung open the door and saw that the room was full of saxophones. "What is this?!"

"It's my *Sax* Room! It's where I play my smooth jazz!" Shivers explained. "The *S* must have fallen off the door!"

Margo groaned. The Roy Scouts were half-way up the rope and moving fast. But then she spotted another door labeled SHARP ROOM. She eagerly looked inside, only to discover that it was filled with shining gold harps.

"Shivers!" she said through gritted teeth. "This isn't a Sharp Room, it's a Harp Room!"

"Oh, *that's* where the *S* went!" Shivers said with relief.

In a last-ditch effort, Margo rushed into the kitchen. She opened the silverware drawer, but it was all pudding spoons. The pantry held nothing but soft foods. Albee was still on the counter finishing his afternoon snack, looking rounder than ever.

"You're no help," Margo said.

"Can't you see I'm eating?" Albee replied, his mouth full of butter.

Margo swung open the freezer door. She pushed past trays of ice cubes with rounded edges—which Shivers had labeled NICE CUBES. Deep in the back corner, she spotted exactly what she needed.

The Roy Scouts were just inches away from the ship's railing when Margo burst out of the kitchen, brandishing a frozen piece of pizza above her head. It was frosted with jagged ice.

"Pizza slice!" she bellowed as she brought down the icy edge and cut straight through the rope. The scouts dropped down into the ocean. They

bobbed on the surface in their bright-orange life vests like oversize goldfish.

"Wow! I didn't expect that to work so well," said Margo.

"It's sharp cheddar!" Shivers called up, still trying to free himself from the life preserver. He'd been keeping that piece of cheese pizza in the freezer for years in the hopes that he would one day overcome his *C*-sickness. But deep down, he knew that would never happen, so he was glad Margo had been able to make good use of it.

Roy pulled the sopping wet scouts back onto

the raft and announced, "Swimming patches for everyone!"

"Hooray!" the scouts cheered.

"Unfortunately, I'm going to have to revoke your climbing patches."

"Aww!" the scouts groaned. They scowled up at Margo.

"If we can't get onto the ship, there's only one thing left to do," said Roy. "Sink it in the name of safety!"

The scouts reached into their pockets and pulled out small red tools.

"Are those pocket knives?!" Shivers edged back in fear.

"You only put a knife in your pocket once before you realize what a bad idea it is," said Roy. "They're pocket sporks!"

The scouts flipped open the tools, revealing small silver spoons with pointy prongs. "The safest fork!" one of the scouts said.

"Or the most dangerous spoon." Shivers grimaced.

"Time to earn your wood-carving patches!" said Roy.

The scouts paddled the raft over to the *Groundhog* and dug their sporks into the side of the ship.

"Not my *Hog*!" Shivers wailed.

Margo looked down at the scouts scraping at the hull in a frenzy. Wood chips were flying

everywhere. Just then, Shivers finally managed to free himself from the life preserver.

Margo pointed to the bag of patches on the floor of the raft. "Shivers! Throw me that bag!"

"But I don't have my throwing patch yet," Shivers protested.

"Just do it!"

Shivers flung the bag into the air with all his strength. It wasn't a lot. But it was enough. Margo reached out and caught the bag by its strap, leaving it dangling over the open ocean.

Roy gasped. The scouts stopped carving at the ship.

"Hand over the pirate or you'll never see your precious patches again," said Margo.

"Never!" said Roy. "We can't let you go to the Bermuda Triangle!" He turned to the scouts. "Sink their ship!"

One of the scouts stood up and stared off into the distance. "But . . . with no patches, there's no point."

"No point?" said Roy. "What about all the great safety tips you've learned?"

"I can't decorate my shirt with safety tips!" another scout said angrily.

The Scouts broke into an angry chant. "NO PATCHES, NO POINT! NO PATCHES, NO POINT!"

"Stop it!" said Roy, but the scouts weren't paying attention. They got louder and louder, and threw their pocket sporks overboard in protest.

Roy threw his hands in the air. "You're throwing away your pocket sporks?! Don't come crying to me the next time you want to eat spaghetti *and* sauce at the same time!"

But it was no use. As is often the case when people are swept up in a great chant, there was no turning back. The scouts rocked the raft, and Roy's eyes widened in fear. He could see his life's work crumbling around him like an overbaked pie.

"Okay, okay! I surrender!" Roy screeched. He clipped an orange life vest around Shivers and plopped him in the water. "Can I have the patches back now, please?!"

"You sure can!" said Margo. She swung the bag around her head, then threw it as far as she could.

The scouts rowed away furiously, trying to get to the bag of patches before it got caught up in the current.

Margo used the anchor to hoist Shivers back onto the *Groundhog.*

"I guess everyone was right," Shivers panted. "The Bermuda Triangle *is* the most dangerous place on earth."

Margo sighed. "Shivers, we're not even half-way there."

And while she corrected course and sailed south, Shivers lay on the deck and screamed.

CHAPTER SEVEN

THE *GROUNDHOG* GLIDED THROUGH the water with a strong wind pushing at the sails. The sun was high in the sky as morning gave way to afternoon. Shivers was exhausted. He had already slid through the sewer and gotten into a catfight, and he was on his way to the most dangerous place on earth. He brought Albee out onto the deck and tried to take his midday nap, but his head was swirling with so many worries that he couldn't even close his eyes.

As the ship approached the Southern Seas, the water began to get rougher. A wave sloshed over the railing, soaking Shivers's slippers.

"AAAGH! MY FEET ARE DROWNING!" he screamed.

Margo was concerned. She knew they were heading toward the world's most treacherous waters, and Shivers already was treating every tiny splash like a tsunami.

"It's time for you to learn how to swim," she announced.

Shivers stood up on his soggy slippers. "Me?! No, thank you." He shook his head. "Swimming is really Albee's department."

Albee swam around his bag in a perfect circle. He truly was an artist.

"Come on, Shivers. If you get lost in the Bermuda Triangle, you're going to have to fend for yourself. There's only so far Albee and I can pull you."

"But I've spent my whole life steering clear of swimming! I sink faster than a brock!"

Margo was confused. "Your brave brother, Brock, is a great swimmer."

"Not *him*! I mean a combination of a brick and a rock!" Shivers explained. "How am I supposed to learn how to swim now?"

"Swimming isn't so hard. It just takes three things," Margo said. "First, you have to kick."

"Well, of course I can do that!" Shivers can-canned across the deck, his feet flying high above his head. "Is the next step singing?" he asked hopefully.

"Nope!" Margo grinned. "It's flailing. And we both know you can do that."

"I can?" Shivers asked.

Margo pulled a sandwich out of her backpack and held it in front of him.

"AAAAAGGGH! A Sand Witch!!! Put it away before it casts a spell on us!!!" Shivers shrieked, flailing his arms so fast he looked like a demented windmill.

"You can kick *and* flail." Margo put the sandwich away. "Now comes the easy part. You just have to hold your breath."

"*Hold* my breath?! That's the craziest thing I've ever heard!" Shivers was flummoxed. He could hold a lot of things–Albee, his favorite mop, and a surprisingly large bowl of banana pudding. He could hold for laughter. He could hold a high note. He'd even spent hours on hold with the ice-cream shop trying to convince them to deliver. But hold his breath? He blurted out, "What if I drop it?!"

Margo laughed. "You won't drop it."

"But I don't even know how much it weighs!"

"What you need is practice." She grabbed one of Shivers's mop buckets and filled it with seawater. She knew that the only way to get Shivers to plunge his head into a bucket of water was to have a reward waiting at the end. So she found a few fuzzy peaches in the kitchen and dropped them into the bucket. "Okay, Shivers! You're going to learn how to hold your breath by bobbing for peaches!"

"My dad loves bobbing for things!" said Shivers. "But maybe it's just because his name is Bob. . . ."

Margo patted Shivers on the back and pointed to the bucket. "Just hold your breath until you bite into a peach, then come back up for air!"

Albee narrowed his eyes. "Why do I get the feeling this is going to end in screeches instead of peaches?"

Shivers took a deep breath and plunged his head into the bucket. But as soon as he felt the water on his freckled face, he skipped straight to the screaming. Water flooded his mouth and shot into his nose. He whipped his head up, sopping, sneezing, and hiccuping hysterically.

"I went down and then I hicced up!" he sputtered.

Albee slapped his fin to his forehead.

Another hefty hiccup rattled through Shivers's fragile body. "How do I–HIC!–get rid of these things?!"

Margo tapped her chin in thought. "Well, there are two options. Either get really scared or hold your breath."

"Those are the two worst options ever! I'm–HIC!–doomed!" he said, throwing his hands in the air.

Margo couldn't help but let out a little laugh.

"What a–HIC!–disaster! I'm never–HIC!–touching water again!" he declared.

At that moment, a gigantic wave crested over the ship, then splashed onto Shivers and soaked the deck. "AAAAGH!" he screamed. "I have so much–HIC!–mopping to do!"

But the mopping would have to wait. Another huge wave slammed into the hull of the *Groundhog*, sending it spinning like a ballerina. Margo stumbled up to the captain's deck as quickly as she could and grabbed the helm.

Shivers picked up Albee and followed Margo. “What’s–HIC!–happening?!”

“Look!” Margo said, pointing straight ahead to a buoy on the water’s surface. Tied to it was a sign that said BERMUDA TRIANGLE AHEAD! TURN BACK NOW!

“We’re almost there!” Margo said.

Shivers wailed, “We’re going to be–HIC!–triangle trash!”

Margo gripped the helm tightly as the ship strained against the churning waves. "Don't worry, Shivers, we'll make it!" she said as she steered them past the buoy.

But then they spotted another sign floating on the water. This one said APPROACHING CERTAIN DEATH!

"AAAGGH!" Shivers screamed. He tightened the straps of his life vest. "I don't know how long this thing will keep me–HIC!–afloat. I need all rubber duckies on deck!" He raced to the bathtub, scooped up as many rubber duckies as he could carry, and stuffed them into his coat pockets. He sprinted back to the captain's deck, picked up Albee's bag, and stared straight into his eyes. "Stay out of the kitchen, Albee! If there's one thing I know, it's that the kitchen sinks!"

By now, the sea was so violent that Margo could barely hold on to the helm. Fierce gusts of wind whipped around her, flapping her ponytail like a flag. The ship reached a third buoy with a sign that read: ENTERING THE BERMUDA TRIANGLE (HOPE YOU KNOW HOW TO SWIM)!

"Shivers, we made it!" Margo shouted. "We're in the Bermuda Triangle!"

"AAAAAAAAAAAGH!" Shivers screamed. "Well, the good news is, I'm so scared that my hiccups are cured."

The ocean swirled around the *Groundhog*. Then a giant wave slapped against the side of the ship, sending Margo, Shivers, and Albee stumbling to the ground.

Margo leaped to her feet and lunged toward the helm, which was spinning like a pinwheel. She grabbed hold of it and tried to gain control, but the current was far too strong. No matter which way she steered, the ship still circled toward the center of the storm.

Meanwhile, Albee's bag was rolling every which way around the main deck.

"Why did I eat so much butter?" Albee groaned.

Shivers chased after him, looking like a madman trying to find his last marble. Just as Shivers got ahold of Albee's bag, a sound came from the sky like the cracking of a giant wooden bat. Rain. It spat down in heavy sheets. Shivers felt certain that he was going to drown.

"The message says that the key to stopping Captain Crook is in a treasure chest!" Margo yelled, holding the helm with all her might. "Shivers, look over the railing! Do you see a treasure chest?"

The rain was coming down harder than ever now. Shivers tried to shield his eyes from the drubbing droplets as he peeked over the edge of the ship and into the sloshing Southern Seas below. The water was a steely gray, empty of any answers. He didn't see a treasure chest, but he did see a streak of light set the waves ablaze . . . and then another, and another.

"All I see down here is lightning!" Shivers shouted.

"What?! Lighting comes from the sky, not the sea!" said Margo.

Shivers shrugged. "Well then, somebody dropped a *lot* of night-lights. . . ."

Just then, a wave as big as a house swelled above the deck. Shivers saw sparks crackling along the crest and he realized that what he was seeing wasn't lightning. And it wasn't night-lights. He had been so, so wrong.

"ELECTRIC EELS!!!"

CHAPTER EIGHT

THE GIANT WAVE CRASHED onto the ship, carrying an army of slimy electric eels with it. They were the most hideous things Shivers had ever seen. They had scaly spotted skin, beady black eyes, and teeth that looked like razor-sharp toothpicks. As the eels slid across the deck, Shivers felt like he was on a plate of the world's most evil spaghetti. He tried to scream, but there were so many eels that all he could do was squeal.

"Margo, these eels are shocking me in more ways than one! Help!"

Margo wanted to help Shivers, but she knew the moment she left the helm the ship would spin out of control. "I have to keep the *Groundhog* on course!" she shouted back.

"Well, I did *not* sign up for this course!" Shivers wailed. An eel slithered between his slippers and wrapped around his ankle. "Take cover!" he screamed. He flung the eel off with one high kick, picked up Albee, and sprinted inside as fast as he could. But the eels skidded in after him on a slide of seawater. They glided into his kitchen and wriggled up onto the counter, zapping everything in their path with eel-ectricity. They sent a spark through the toaster, and it popped up and down wildly, springing burnt bread onto the floor. The

microwave buzzed on, setting off explosions of popcorn inside. The blender whirred to life, splattering blueberry smoothie everywhere.

"Why do I preload all my kitchen appliances?!" Shivers screamed. He leaped across the kitchen and ducked down to avoid getting a faceful of flying food. "Let's store ourselves in the pantry," he said to Albee. He opened the pantry door, but the eels were already inside, sizzling his snacks and toasting his oats. "Eels in my meals!!!" Shivers squawked.

Shivers slammed the pantry door and dashed down the hall to his bedroom. There was no escape. The eels followed at his heels, sparking on every light they passed. And in Shivers's bedroom, that was a *lot* of lights. Along with the standard collection of night-lights, reading lights, lamp lights, and dance lights, there were high-voltage safety lights under the bed and in the closet. Suddenly, the whole ship was so brightly lit, it looked like a firefly on a trampoline.

The eels zapped on the clock next to Shivers's bed, setting off the alarm. Shivers covered his ears, but then the eels crawled over the stereo, and it began to play rock and roll–which was just the sound of rocks rolling around. Shivers usually listened to it very quietly to help him get to sleep, but now it was blaring at full volume, and it sounded like he was in the middle of an avalanche.

Shivers stuck his head out of the porthole and screamed, "Margo!! Do something!! The eels are winning!!"

Margo knew that Shivers was right. Eels were all over the captain's deck. They tried to slither onto her legs, but she

hopped over them with expert precision. (All that time she'd spent jumping rope at recess was really paying off.) But every wave that hit the ship brought more and more eels on board. For every eel she dodged, two more showed up. Margo knew she would have to do something drastic.

"Shivers!" Margo shouted. "Hold on tight!"

"To what?! An eel?!" said Shivers.

"I'm steering us into the waves!"

"Are you crazy? The ship will flip right over!"

"That's the whole point!" said Margo. "We have to face our fears head-on!"

Shivers thought fast and wrapped himself as best he could around his bedpost while holding on tightly to Albee's bag.

Margo wrenched the helm as hard as she could, steering the ship directly into the waves. A massive swell scooped up the *Groundhog* and lifted it into the air. Shivers shrieked as the ship teetered on its side, nearly toppling over entirely. The eels poured out through the open porthole, zipping and zapping, then did an electric slide right off the edge of the deck and dropped back into the ocean.

"Hooray!" Margo cheered.

"Hoor-AAAGGH!" Shivers shouted. It was as close to a cheer as Margo could hope for.

But the celebration lasted about as long as a balloon in a cactus store. The waves were too strong. The ocean was steering now. The *Groundhog* whipped and twisted. It was impossible to see where they were heading.

"I told you we shouldn't have come here!" Shivers shouted to Margo. "The Bermuda Triangle is the scariest place in the entire world!"

And with that, the ship caught the crest of a giant wave and nearly flipped upside down. All Margo could do was hold on for dear life, while Shivers held on for fear life. But the force was too strong. Shivers, Margo, and Albee were flung from the ship. As they sailed through the air, Shivers wailed, "It was nice knowing you! Except for all the terrifying adventures!" And then–

WHAM!

They landed on a sandy beach. The sky was blue. The sun was shining. Relaxing island music filled the air. Shivers and Margo rubbed the grit from their eyes and saw that they were surrounded by people in brightly colored swimsuits holding big icy drinks. A woman in a straw hat stepped forward. She waved at them with a huge smile on her face and announced, "Welcome to the Bermuda Triangle!"

SHIVERS, MARGO, AND ALBEE all had the same dumbfounded look on their faces.

The woman in the straw hat pulled them to their feet. "I'm Dana, the events planner. But everyone here calls me the party captain!"

The people around her shouted, "Woo! Party captain!"

Finally, Margo managed to gain control of her mouth. "I'm Margo. This is my best friend, Shivers, and his first mate, Albee."

"We're *so* glad you're here!" Dana pulled all three of them in for a warm hug. Then she

turned to the people around her. "Okay, everyone, get back to having fun!"

The crowd cheered again and scattered across the beach. They danced to steel-drum music played by a live band. They splashed in the crystal-clear water and zipped around on Jet Skis. They filled up their plates with delicious-looking food from a giant buffet. Just a few yards from the sand was a bustling resort, complete with a golf course, tennis courts, horseback riding, yoga classes, and a sparkling swimming pool.

Shivers shook his head in disbelief. "*This* is the Bermuda Triangle?!"

"It sure is," said Dana, slurping from a straw crammed into a coconut shell.

"But I thought the Bermuda Triangle was the most dangerous place on earth! No one who comes here ever returns!" said Shivers.

"Because no one who comes here ever *wants* to return," Dana explained. "The Bermuda Triangle is paradise!"

She led Shivers, Margo, and Albee along the beach. "One way or another, all these people got lost on the open ocean and ended up here. Then, when they saw how great it was, they decided to stay forever!" She pointed to a group playing beach volleyball. "They were on a cruise ship that took a wrong turn on the way to Mexico."

A guy in bright-red swim trunks hit the ball over the net, then turned to them with a big grin on his face. "I've been here for three years . . . or is it four? Who cares?"

Dana continued, "Fishing vessels, whale-watching tours, oil rigs–you name it! All kinds of ships crash-land in the Bermuda Triangle."

"I was in a relation-ship and I never looked back!" said one of the steel-drum players, then he burst into peals of laughter.

"He makes that joke *every* day," Dana whispered.

As they walked past the buffet table, Shivers's stomach growled and Margo's eyes widened at the heaping platters of food. There were fruit cakes, cupcakes, and crab cakes . . . coffee, cake, *and* coffee cake.

Shivers pointed to a tray of almond-crusted donuts. "Do you have any donuts with no nuts?" he asked.

"Of course we do! Go nuts!" said Dana, handing him a donut with sprinkles. Then she gestured to a spread of breaded chicken. "How about some chicken fingers?"

Shivers leaped back and screeched. "Those chickens must have had huge hands!"

Margo helped herself to a cupcake. "Where did all of this come from?"

"Ships land here constantly, carrying all kinds of stuff!" Dana put her arm around a tall man in blue overalls. "Just last week, Carl here crashed his cargo ship filled with gourmet food and tambourines!" She picked up a tambourine from a basket and shook it above her head.

"Best thing that ever happened to me!" said Carl.

Dana nodded. "The only thing we had to throw out was that giant crate of eels."

Shivers and Margo locked eyes and shuddered.

Dana continued, "You never know what might wash ashore in the Bermuda Triangle. Just the other day, I found this box on the beach! Must have fallen off a ship by accident!" She picked up a weathered, salt-stained treasure chest from the sand. Carved into the wood was the same symbol that was on the flag of Captain Crook's Ship: an iron lock.

"Now I use it to store my prizes!" said Dana.

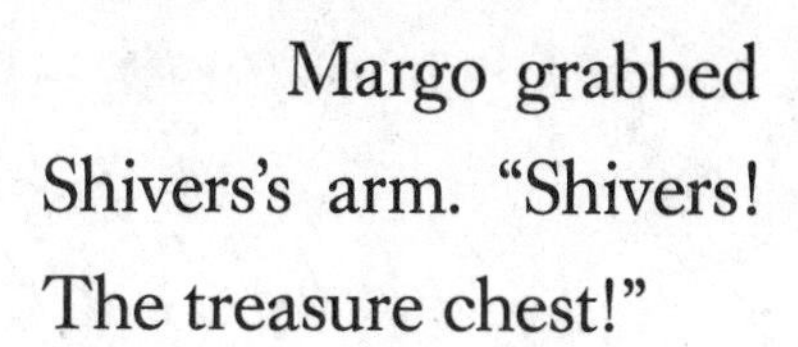

Margo grabbed Shivers's arm. "Shivers! The treasure chest!"

Shivers gasped and reached out toward the treasure chest, but Dana swatted his hand away.

"I don't think so!" she said. "If you want a prize, you have to win a game. And you're just in time for my favorite–limbo!"

"But–"

Before Margo or Shivers could say another word, Dana started banging on her tambourine as loud as she could, shouting "LIMBO TIME!" over and over again. Everyone on the beach abruptly stopped what they were doing and eagerly formed a line, their faces brimming with anticipation.

Margo turned to Shivers. "The key to stopping

Captain Crook must be in that treasure chest! We have to win the limbo!"

"I don't even know what limbo is," Shivers said nervously.

"IT'S THE GREATEST GAME ON EARTH!" Dana shouted. "You stand in a long line, then you walk under a stick!"

Shivers was confused. "And then what?"

"If you don't touch the stick, you get to stand in line *again*! You'll love it!" She grabbed Shivers and Margo's hands and pulled them over to the group.

Margo knew how much Shivers hated lines. Droplets of sweat were already forming on his forehead. She could see from the noses on his bunny slippers that his toes were twitching. And then they brought out the broom. Dana held one end while Carl from the cargo ship held the other end.

"AAAAGH!" Shivers screamed. "Not a broom!"

"Shivers, how can you be afraid of brooms?" Margo asked. "You love mops!"

"It's not the same thing at all!" said Shivers. "That's like comparing apples and oranges, peaches and plums, popcorn and . . . unpopped corn!" He winced. "A broom is like a mop that shriveled up and died!"

Shivers tried to step out of the line, but Margo pulled him back in. "Come on, Shivers, we can do this! We *need* to do this!"

Shivers let out a deep sigh as the line began to move. One by one, the happy partygoers wiggled under the broomstick to the beat of the steel-drum music. Some were just able to duck their heads under, while others collapsed in the sand, laughing. As Margo and Shivers moved closer to the front, Shivers's broom doom swept him into a frenzy.

"I've got to stay as far away from that thing as possible!" he squeaked.

"That's the whole point," Margo said. She bent backward and waddled under the broom. But it was harder than it looked, especially while carrying Albee in his bag. Margo lost her balance and came crashing down in the sand.

"Oh, no! Albee pulled you down!" Shivers cried.

"It's the water weight!" Albee huffed, swimming in a circle.

Margo stood up and dusted herself off. "It's up to you, Shivers!"

Shivers took a deep breath and tiptoed over to the broomstick. As he got closer and closer, he was filled with terror at the sight of the wooden handle and the spiky bundle of straw. His eyes widened. "The only thing a broom is good for is giving a scarecrow a high five!" He threw his head back and sprinted under as fast as he could.

"I did it! I did it!" Shivers cheered. "What do I do now?"

"Get back in line!" said Dana. "Isn't this fun?!"

With every round, Dana and Carl lowered the broomstick, and more and more partygoers got out of the game. But not Shivers. A lifetime of screeching and flailing had made him quite

flexible, and he was so afraid that the broom might give him a splinter that he avoided it at all costs. Soon, the line had dwindled down to just Shivers and a circus performer named Pierre whose big tent had caught the wind during storm season and sailed him all the way to the Bermuda Triangle. The broom was barely a foot off the ground. Pierre stretched backward as far as he could. But apparently the circus isn't what it used to be. He couldn't get low enough and his head hit the broom.

"I've been conked!" Pierre cried.

Shivers just had to clear the broom one more time and he would win the limbo. The crowd looked on to see if his scrawny legs would bend under the pressure. They chanted, "How low can you go? How low can you go?"

Shivers bent back as far as he could. For all the times he'd been scared stiff, his spine still had some bend to it. As he wobbled under the broom, a single bristle nearly brushed the brim of his feathered pirate cap.

Margo thought fast. "Shivers!" she yelled. "A broom is a witch's favorite mode of transportation!"

Shivers arched back even farther and screamed, "THIS IS AS LOW AS I GO!" He wiggled his way past the broom with nothing but sheer terror keeping him up.

"We have a winner!" Dana announced. The crowd burst into applause.

"It was a clean sweep!" said Albee. But his wit went unappreciated.

Dana held out the treasure chest, and Shivers looked inside. It was packed with junk. He pushed aside giant pink plastic sunglasses, feather boas, and bags of candy. Finally, all the way at the bottom, he found a big silver key.

"I GOT IT!" Shivers declared, waving the key above his head.

"I didn't even know that was in there." Dana laughed. "Everyone always goes for the giant sunglasses."

Margo rushed over to Shivers and hugged him with joy. "You did it!" She placed the silver key securely in her pocket. "Now let's get out of here!"

A confused murmur rippled through the crowd.

Dana's face fell. "You're . . . leaving? But you just got here! The fun is just getting started! I know—let's play Twister!"

"What's Twister?" Shivers asked.

"It's a game where everyone gets tangled in a big knot until they fall over," said Dana. "You'll love it!"

"We *really* have to go," said Margo.

Pierre pointed at Shivers. "I know the problem! He's too tense!"

"What you need is a relaxing massage," said Dana.

"What's a massage?" Shivers asked, backing away.

"Everybody grabs your arms, legs, and back, then pinches you as hard as they can. You'll love it!"

The partygoers held up their hands and closed in on Shivers, looking like a pack of bears about to maul him. They mashed his measly muscles and smooshed his squishy shoulders. One lady massaged Shivers's feet with her hands while another massaged his hands with her feet.

Margo could tell that Shivers didn't find this very relaxing, because he was crying, laughing, and screaming all at the same time. It sounded like this:

Margo grabbed Shivers by the arms and pulled him out of the crowd. She felt like she was dragging a giant noodle.

"Thanks, Margo," Shivers panted. "That was awful. The message in a bottle was terrifying, but at least it wasn't a *massage* in a bottle."

Dana hurried over to Shivers. "You're still not having fun? I know just what you need!" She darted away, then returned leading a giant horse by its reins. "A soothing horseback ride!"

"Huh?" Shivers sat up and looked at the horse, which was snorting and stomping. Its dark eyes were as big as blackberry pies.

"It's the most fun thing in the world!" said Dana. "We'll hoist you up onto the hairy back of a two-thousand-pound animal, then send it running down the beach while you try your best not to fall off! YOU'LL LOVE IT!"

Shivers let out a scream so high-pitched it sounded like air escaping from a balloon. Then he tore off across the beach in such a panic that he looked like a balloon escaping from air. He took a sharp turn and ran toward the swimming pool. As soon as he burst through the gate, the lifeguard barked, "NO RUNNING NEAR THE POOL!" and blew his whistle as hard as he could.

Unfortunately, right next to the lifeguard was a woman reading in a lounge chair. The shrill noise was so alarming that she screamed and flung her book in the air. It landed in front of a tennis coach who was pushing a cart full of balls toward the court. The book snagged one of the wheels and tipped the cart over. Bright green tennis balls spilled out everywhere. It looked like a lime tree had exploded.

The tennis balls rolled down to the bottom of a grassy hill where there was a small group of people in the middle of a yoga class. Unfortunately, it was a yoga class for beginners, so everyone had terrible balance. They tripped on the tennis balls and crashed into each other like sweaty dominoes. The yoga teacher tried her best to stay on her feet but she stumbled backward and fell into a golfer who was teeing off on the first hole of the golf course. The golfer swung his club wildly and sent the ball sailing off in the wrong direction.

The golf ball flew over the beach all the way to the ocean, where it bounced right off a Jet Skier's head. The Jet Skier teetered from side to side.

"Did it just get dizzy in here?" he said. Then he fell into the water, leaving the Jet Ski without a driver. The out-of-control Jet Ski zoomed up onto the beach. It plowed through the volleyball net, ripped down the hammocks, and then collided with the tiki torches, which tipped over and set the entire buffet table ablaze, melting the ice cream, burning the biscuits, and over-roasting

the chicken. The broomstick got burned, the steel drums were smoldering, and even the basket of tambourines was torched to a crisp. The party was officially over.

Shivers, Margo, and Albee stood in stunned silence, staring at the destruction.

Dana marched over to the pool, clutching her straw hat. "What. Have. You. Done?!"

"Um . . ." Shivers slowly backed away.

Every single person on the island scowled at him with fury.

Margo called to Shivers, "I know I say this every time we go on an adventure, but . . . RUN!"

They both sprinted toward the *Groundhog* as fast as they could, kicking up clouds of sand behind them. The angry mob chased after them.

"Margo, help!" Shivers pointed down at his slippers. "My bunnies can't go any faster!"

Margo spotted the horse up ahead, grazing on a patch of golf-course grass. "Then we're going to need a faster animal!" She grabbed Shivers's hand and jumped onto the horse.

"Margo!" Shivers wailed as they landed in the saddle. "Didn't you see the rules at the pool? No horseplay!"

Margo kicked her heels and shouted, "Giddyup!"

"No! Giddydown!" Shivers screeched as the horse bolted across the sand.

Margo held on to the horse's mane. Shivers held on to Margo's ponytail. Albee held on to the hope that one day he'd just get to relax in his bowl. The horse skidded to a stop in front of

the *Groundhog*. Shivers and Margo raced onto the ship and raised the sails as quickly as they could just as the mob reached the edge of the shore.

As the *Groundhog* crashed through the waves, Shivers and Margo looked back at the crowd. The expressions on their faces suddenly shifted from anger to confusion. It was like a spell was being lifted.

Dana blinked and shook her head. "Wait a minute. How long have we been here?"

"I don't know! I was so caught up in all the fun!" said Carl from the cargo ship.

“I haven’t seen my wife in months!” one guy said.

“I missed my kid’s graduation!” said another.

“Oh no!” a woman cried. “My parking meter expired six years ago!”

The crowd dispersed. Everyone returned to their ships and prepared to head back to wherever it was they came from.

Back on the *Groundhog*, Margo steered straight out of the Bermuda Triangle. Actually, it wasn’t really straight. It was a twisted, curvy, wobbly, swervy way out–anything she could do to keep the boat as far away from all the eels as possible.

CHAPTER TEN

AS THEY SAILED BACK to New Jersey, Margo and Albee had the wind at their backs while Shivers had the wind in his face. But that's because he was facing backward. If he faced forward, he might have to face his fears, and that was one ugly face. Earlier today, he was certain that the Bermuda Triangle would be the most terrifying place he went, but now Margo wanted to go someplace even scarier: Captain Crook's ship.

Margo could see that Shivers was terrified.

"Don't worry, Shivers! We have the key to stopping Captain Crook!" she said, pulling the silver key out of her pocket. "All we have to do is sneak onto his ship, figure out what this key opens, and defeat him! The hard part is over!"

"Well, then when does the soft part start?" Shivers moaned. He really wanted to take a nap.

It wasn't long before they heard the clucking of New Jersey's famous sewer chickens and they knew they were close to home.

"If Captain Crook is going to attack New Jersey, he must be around here somewhere," said Margo. She took a pair of binoculars out of her backpack and handed them to Shivers. "Any sign of him?"

Shivers looked through the binoculars and screamed, "AAAGH! A tiny ship!"

Margo sighed and flipped the binoculars around.

"AAAAGH! A HUGE ship!" he screeched.

Captain Crook's ship was anchored just up ahead. Shivers recognized the rotting black hull and the iron lock painted on the sails. "Margo, this is a bad idea! If Captain Crook catches us, he'll feed us to the jellyfish. . . . We'll be sleeping with the stingrays. . . . We'll go to whale jail!"

“Shivers, we’ve made it this far.” She grabbed him by the shoulders. “Remember, if you want to conquer your fears, you have to face them head-on. And I’ve got a plan. But first, we have to disguise the ship. Quick, Shivers! Lower the flag!”

Shivers lowered the *Groundhog*’s flag, which was a picture of a big smiley face, while Margo grabbed a marker from her backpack. She scribbled out the smile and replaced it with a frown.

Shivers shook his head. “I do *not* like the message that sends.”

“It’s only temporary,” said Margo. “If we’re going to defeat the people-hating pirates, I’m afraid we’re going to have to pretend to *be* people-hating pirates.”

“But that looked like a permanent marker to me,” said Shivers.

Margo ignored Shivers and turned her attention to the gleaming grand piano in the middle of the deck. “The piano is too suspicious. We need to cover it up.”

“I’ll get my shower curtain,” Shivers said proudly. “I’m never using it again anyway.”

As Shivers draped the shower curtain over the grand piano, Margo raised the new flag back up the mast. “Okay, we’ve disguised the ship. Now, we have to disguise me–”

“I’ve still got my peacock costume from last Halloween!” Shivers said excitedly.

“As a *pirate*, Shivers.” For as fierce as Margo was on the inside, she still looked like a ten-year-old kid on the outside, with her sneakers, T-shirt, and bouncy brown ponytail. “Do you have any extra pirate clothes?”

“Just these,” Shivers said, pointing to the clothes he was wearing. “The rest are all jammies.”

“Okay, then. I’ll have to get creative.” She took off her backpack and dropped it at the helm.

Then she flew down the stairs to the main deck and dashed into the kitchen.

Shivers followed, curious to see what she was going to do and also hoping to grab a quick snack in the process. Margo grabbed a dish towel and tied it around her head like a bandanna. Then she found a box of raisins in the pantry.

"AAAGH! Zombie grapes!" Shivers screamed. "What are you going to do with those?"

"Check it out," she said, shoving the raisins onto her teeth so it looked like they had rotted right out of her mouth.

"Gross"–Shivers recoiled–"but effective. You're really starting to look like a pirate."

"Speaking of looking . . ." Margo said. She looked in the fridge and found a piece of baloney, which she taped over her left eye so it looked like an eye patch . . . kind of. It would have to do.

She put on her most menacing face and marched back outside as they were drifting into the shadow of Captain Crook's enormous ship. They were just a sword's slice away from the black rotting hull. It was anchored to the ocean floor, rocking back and forth slowly.

Shivers's teeth began to clatter with concern. "What if Captain Crook sees us?"

"Don't worry, Shivers. It looks like the coast is clear," said Margo.

There wasn't a pirate in sight on the deck of the ship. Margo hooked a rope onto the railing, grabbed Albee's bag, and climbed aboard in no time.

Shivers followed, gripping the rope so tightly that his knuckles turned white. Once he was close enough, Margo grabbed him by his pirate coat and yanked him on board.

She looked around the empty deck. "Where's Captain Crook's evil pirate crew?"

Shivers clasped his hands together. "Maybe they decided they don't want to be pirates after all! Maybe they gave up and got new jobs like teachers and bankers and popcorn-ball makers! Why don't we sail to the beach and check?"

Just then, Margo spotted movement at the helm, all the way at the other end of the deck. It was Captain Crook. His long, crooked fingers cast long, crooked shadows in the evening sunlight. Next to him was his first mate, Spitball. Her wiry hair stuck out in every direction and even from all the way across the deck, Shivers could see the menacing look in her wild eyes. They were deep in conversation, pointing at the coastline.

Margo pulled Shivers behind a barrel of old fish carcasses that said LEFTOVERS. "Get down, or we'll be spotted!" she whispered.

"Oh no! I never want to be spotted!" Shivers

squeaked. "I wouldn't mind being striped, though. I love zebras."

Margo wasn't listening. "Now's our chance! Let's make our way inside and start searching!"

Margo, Shivers, and Albee scampered across the deck, trying to stay as low as they could. Margo opened a rickety door, and they entered a long, dark hallway. The only light came from a flickering candle that was placed inside a skull.

"Yikes." Shivers shuddered. "This guy needs a new decorator." He peered into umbrella stand that said USED SWORDS. "Wow, the crew must make a lot of hamburgers. Their swords are all covered in ketchup!"

"That's not ketchup . . ." said Albee.

"Over here!" Margo said, standing in front of a door at the end of the hall. Carved into the rotting wood were the words CAPTAIN CROOK'S QUARTERS—COME IN! (IF YOU WANT TO DIE!).

Margo took a deep breath and slowly pushed open the door.

Inside, there was a large wooden desk topped with pelican quills and squid ink. Captain Crook's bed was covered with a salmon-skin quilt, and the bedposts were made of blue coral.

Shivers shook his head. "This guy doesn't care about the Pirate Code at all! Rule number fourteen is: Don't disturb the coral!"

In the corner of the room was a large wooden chest of drawers. And every single drawer was secured with a heavy metal lock.

"Jackpot," Margo said with a grin. She turned to Shivers and held up the silver key. "The key has to unlock one of those drawers. I'm going to get to work. You stand guard."

Shivers put his hands on his hips. "Do you mind if I sit guard? I'm really tired."

But just then, they heard heavy footsteps approaching.

"Captain Crook!" Shivers gasped.

"Hide!" Margo whispered.

Margo and Shivers darted out of the room and ducked into a closet across the hall. They closed the door behind them just as the footsteps entered the hallway.

In the dim light streaming through the porthole, Shivers could see that they were inside a supply closet. The walls were lined with jars full of jellies and jams, grains, sweets, and salted meats. The whole place smelled like rotting tuna.

On the floor was a giant barrel that said EXTRA-EXTRA-LARGE FISH FLAKES.

"What are those for?" Shivers whispered as quietly as he possibly could.

"I don't know, but it's making me hungry," said Albee.

Margo held a finger to her lips. She froze, trying not to make a sound as the footsteps walked past Captain Crook's quarters and stopped right outside the supply closet. As the knob began to turn, Shivers hoped this was all a terrible nightmare and it was time to wake up. Margo just hoped that the baloney on her face looked enough like a real eye patch to fool a real pirate.

CHAPTER ELEVEN

THE DOOR TO THE closet swung open. But it wasn't Captain Crook standing in the doorway. It was a man Shivers and Margo had never seen before. He had black stringy hair and a wispy goatee.

"AAAGH!" Shivers screamed.

"AAAGH!" the man screamed back.

"AHOY!" Margo shouted, trying to cover their tracks.

The man eyed them suspiciously. "What are you doin' in here?"

"Um . . . We be lookin' for a snack before the big attack!" said Margo.

The man grinned, revealing a mouthful of splintery wooden teeth. "You must be new recruits. I'm the ship's cook." He extended a filthy hand. "Everyone calls me Weasel."

Shivers grimaced. "That's a weird nickname."

"Well, my real name's Ship Scum Jr., so I don't really mind."

Shivers shook Weasel's hand. Actually, he just grabbed it, but because he was shivering so much, it felt like a handshake.

"You're late for tea!" Weasel collected a few murky jars from the shelves. "Follow me. The rest of the crew is below deck. I'll introduce you to the bloodthirsty horde."

Margo desperately wanted to get back into the captain's quarters so she could try the key in the locks. "We–we don't have time," she sputtered.

"Nonsense! We've got all the time in the world! We're all just bobbin' here until we get the order to attack. Cap'n Crook and that foul-mouthed Spitball be drawin' up the plans as we speak." Weasel narrowed his eyes at Shivers and Margo. "You wouldn't be doin' anything without orders from the cap'n, would you?"

Shivers and Margo shook their heads frantically.

"I thought not," said Weasel.

Seeing no other choice, they followed Weasel down the hall toward a narrow staircase. Shivers lagged behind Margo, gripping Albee's bag and trying his best not to scream his brains out.

As they rounded the corner, Shivers tapped Margo on the shoulder and whispered, "This might come as a surprise to you, but I'm *very* scared right now! How am I supposed to blend in with a brutal pack of pirates?!"

Margo whispered back, "Just say the scariest thing that comes to mind."

Shivers thought for a moment. "When a butterfly is born, it starts out as a gross, hairy worm!"

"On second thought, say the *opposite* of what comes to mind."

"Okay . . ." He took a deep breath. "This is a great idea, and nothing can possibly go wrong."

They descended the stairs, and at the bottom, they found themselves in a dank, windowless room. The walls were covered in rusted swords, and a tangle of mossy fishing nets hung from the ceiling. A chandelier of sagging wax candles cast a sickly yellow light throughout the room. The entire place was packed with pirates shouting at each other, arm wrestling, and arguing over who had the sharpest hook. Many of them had surly parrots on their shoulders, preening, squawking, and pooping everywhere. There was even live music, but that turned out to be just one pirate in the corner playing a wooden spoon on his wooden leg.

"Welcome to the Harpoon Saloon," Weasel said with a smile. "At least that's what I call it. Everyone else calls it 'Weasel's gross basement.'"

He pulled a splinter from his teeth and flicked it to the floor. "LISTEN UP!"

The pirates fell silent and stared at Shivers and Margo.

"We've got two new villainous recruits joinin' our ranks! They're ready to rip up the Pirate Code and wipe out every soul on the Eastern Seaboard!" Weasel bellowed.

The pirates grunted their approval and rapped their rocky knuckles on the tables.

Margo spoke up in her snarliest voice. "The name be MAAAAARRRG-O! Slaughterer of squids!"

The crew stomped their feet and cheered.

Then Shivers cleared his throat and whimpered, "And I'm Shivers! The pirate who's . . . afraid of nothing!"

The man with the wooden leg hoisted himself up, looking suspiciously at Shivers's feet. "What's with them slippers?" he growled.

What isn't *with these slippers?* Shivers thought. He loved bunnies, he loved soft shoes, and these were easily the trendiest fashion choice he'd made all year! But he stuck with Margo's advice.

"These are two rabid rabbits that I killed and stuffed . . . with my feet!" he said, raising his arm in the air.

The pirates looked around at each other, nodding enthusiastically. Even Margo was stunned.

But the man with the wooden leg still wasn't convinced. "Where's yer parrot?" he sneered.

Shivers hated parrots. His parents had once given him a parrot. Every time he screamed, the parrot screamed right back. Then he would scream again, and the parrot would scream again. It ended up being ten days of straight screaming. It was a dark time. Shivers knew he couldn't tell these pirates that.

"I ate my parrot!" he blurted out.

The whole crowd gasped.

Then Shivers held up Albee. "That's why I got this fish! Because he never talks back."

"Never!" said Albee, but his sarcasm was lost on the room.

Everyone looked at Shivers with quiet respect, wondering where this tough pirate had come from, and whether they should consider getting fish for pets.

The pirates heard the sound of footsteps descending the stairs, and they fell silent. Captain Crook stepped into view. In the dusty light, he was even more terrifying than Shivers had remembered. His long blood-red pirate coat draped behind him like a shadow. The keys on the chain around his neck clinked against each other like bones. Spitball was right behind him. Her hair looked like a bird's nest had exploded on top of her head, and when she smiled, Shivers shuddered at the sight of her missing front teeth.

"Cap'n Crook!" Weasel exclaimed. "I didn't know you were coming. Let me pour you some tea!" He sloshed some sludgy green liquid into a copper cup.

As Weasel handed Captain Crook his tea, Shivers and Margo slunk to the back of the room and slouched down in a shadowy corner so they wouldn't be seen.

Captain Crook cleared his throat. "My fellow scalawags! The time be nearin' for us to start our gruesome attack on the landlubbin' fools of New Jersey."

The pirates grunted their approval. Shivers could see Margo's ears getting red with anger. Weasel wove his way through the room, serving tea. He handed Shivers and Margo two slime-filled cups.

Captain Crook continued, "We'll finally free ourselves from the shackles of the Pirate Code and take our place in history as the roughest, toughest crew on the face of the earth!"

"Hear, hear!" the pirates cheered.

"Our ship is stocked with swords so sharp you

could cut a man's head off twice before he even noticed. Our crew be horrid and hideous, not a trustworthy one of you in the bunch!"

Spitball stepped forward and spat on the ground. "And Janet has never been hungrier!" she bellowed, her piercing voice scratching the walls like glass.

The pirates leaped to their feet. They roared with excitement, shook their hooks, and stomped their feet.

Shivers turned to Margo and whispered, "Who is *Janet*?"

But Margo didn't have an answer.

Captain Crook raised his drink in the air and roared, "Those ignorant landlubbers won't see us coming until we string them up by their belt loops!"

Margo was growing more enraged by the second.

A round pirate whose coat buttons were almost bursting leaped up from her chair and bellowed, "We'll shake 'em till their eyeballs rattle and gold falls from their pockets!"

The pirate with the wooden leg clanked his spoon. "I'll finally get to replace my wooden leg with a real human leg!"

Weasel jumped up on a table and shouted, "To Cap'n Crook!"

The pirates repeated at a fever pitch, "To Captain Crook!" Then everyone took big gulps from their cups.

Margo whispered to Shivers, "Let's drink this tea and get out of here!"

They drained their cups in one quick slurp, and their mouths were filled with a thick salty bitterness that crawled down their throats like a wet bug.

Margo gritted her raisin-covered teeth.

"What kind of tea *is* this?" Shivers shuddered.

"Two parts algae, one part ship sludge; blend with boiled barnacles, and add a dash of love," Weasel said proudly. "I call it Sea Tea!"

As soon as Shivers heard those words, the boiled brew sitting inside his stomach became a supercharged slew of slush and immediately spewed itself straight up and out of his mouth. It flew across the room, splashing and splattering everywhere.

Captain Crook picked a string of algae off his eye patch. "I've only met one pirate who gets seasick before." He marched over to the dark corner. "Shivers the Pirate Who's Afraid of Everything." He yanked the baloney eye patch right off Margo's face. "And his little friend, Margo."

Spitball gasped.

The pirate with the wooden leg shot up from his chair. "What?! You said your names were Shivers the Pirate Who's Afraid of Nothing and MAAAAARRRG-O! I've never felt so lied to before in me life!"

"These aren't real pirates," Captain Crook announced. "They're imposters!"

The crew drew their rusty blades from their belts and pointed them at Shivers and Margo. Shivers let out a long, low wheeze. Margo knew there was a scream deep down in there that was too scared to come out.

Captain Crook narrowed his eyes and widened his nostrils. "Now what in a squid's name are you doing on my ship?"

Margo was at the end of her rope. She balled up her fists, stood up as tall as she could, and said, "We're here to stop you from attacking the innocent people of New Jersey!"

"*You?* Stop *me*?" Captain Crook let out a low chuckle like a frog choking.

Margo continued, "Why are you attacking the land, anyway?"

Captain Crook smiled. "Because it'll be so easy. People don't know how to fight. They're nothing but a bunch of soda-slurpin', soft-bellied, land-livin' lumps." He pointed at Shivers. "And scaredy-cats."

Shivers held up his hand. "I'll admit, I am scared of cats."

Captain Crook began pacing back and forth. "As soon as my crew gets their hooks and hands on the unsuspecting beach biscuits that live in New Jersey, we'll shake 'em out like dusty rugs and take everything they've got . . . like this!"

Captain Crook snapped his fingers. Spitball lunged at Shivers, grabbed him by his bunny slippers, and turned him upside down, cackling like a crow at a comedy show.

"AAAGH!" Shivers screamed, gripping Albee's bag tightly so he wouldn't drop him.

As Spitball shook Shivers, a cascade of clutter came clattering down from his coat pockets onto the rotting wood floor. There was a plastic spoon, two deflated floaties, four popcorn kernels, and either some pillow stuffing or some old marshmallows–it was hard to tell.

But Captain Crook was fixated on the folded piece of paper that came fluttering down last. He picked it up. "What have we here? 'Cheese Curd Night.'"

It was the flyer that Police Chief Clomps'n' Stomps had given to Shivers earlier that day. As Captain Crook's eyes skimmed the rest of the page, his smile grew so wide that Shivers could see the seaweed stuck between his teeth. Captain Crook held the flyer high above his head and turned to his crew. "This is the opportunity we've been waiting for! All of New Jersey will be gathered on this pier, their mouths so stuffed with stringy cheese they won't even be able to scream when they see us! We attack tonight!"

The entire crew cheered and banged their copper mugs on the tables in agreement.

Margo's stomach sank like a sock full of rocks. Spitball dropped Shivers to the ground.

"Ouch!" Shivers cried as he landed feathered-pirate-cap-first.

“I’m sorry,” Captain Crook said with a sneer. “Where are my manners?”

“I’ve been wondering that all day,” Shivers groaned.

“As a thank-you for this most valuable information, let’s introduce our new friends to Janet.”

“Who is Janet?!” Shivers asked for the second time.

“Better seen than said,” Captain Crook replied. “Tie ’em up and walk ’em to the plank!”

“Uh, never mind! I don’t need to know who Janet is!” said Shivers.

But he didn’t have a choice. Spitball tied his hands behind his back while Weasel seized Margo. They led them up to the deck.

The rest of the crew followed, falling over each other with excitement.

Spitball and Weasel shoved Shivers and Margo onto a wooden plank that stretched out from the edge of the ship.

Captain Crook pulled a sword from his belt and growled, "Simon says walk."

Margo scowled at him. "I hate that game."

"It's not a game!" Captain Crook shouted. "My first name is Simon. Now, go!"

Shivers and Margo edged out onto the plank.

Shivers's teeth chattered with terror. "Margo, what are we going to do?! This is the only time when running away from our problems would make the situation *worse*!"

But Margo didn't have an answer. There was no choice but to put one foot in front of the other until they reached the end of the plank.

Captain Crook let out a piercing whistle, then shouted, "Oh, Janet! Snack time!"

Albee grimaced. "I don't like the sound of that."

Shivers and Margo looked down at the churning waves. Just below the frothy surface they saw a pale-green blur. Then, suddenly, a giant beast sprang out of the water with an ear-shattering screech. It had teeth like sharpened traffic cones; a wide, flat head; and a long, scaly neck. Thrashing

its broad flippers against the water with the force of a thousand belly flops, it snapped its jaw just inches from Shivers's and Margo's toes.

Shivers screamed with all the strength his little lungs could muster, "SEA MONSTER!"

THE SEA MONSTER REARED its head, looking as hungry as Shivers did every morning before breakfast. The pirate crew hollered and cheered and drooled with anticipation. They slapped each other on the back–which really hurt for the ones who got slapped with hooks.

Captain Crook called down to the monster, "Janet! I brought you some appetizers before tonight's main course!"

Janet opened her mouth wide. Slobber dotted her sharp teeth.

Margo looked at Shivers. "I'm sorry I got us into this mess."

Shivers looked back at her. "Deep down I always knew I'd be eaten by a sea monster."

"It's a fish-eat-fish world," said Albee.

Captain Crook leaped onto the plank, a dastardly grin smeared across his unpleasant face. He held out his rusty sword at arm's length. "It's called walking the plank, not *talking* the plank! Now get moving!"

Shivers and Margo began to take their last step, when Spitball's high-pitched screech cut through the air. "WAIT!"

Captain Crook looked back at her. "What say you, Spitball? This better be good."

"On the contrary, Captain! It's evil!" said Spitball.

"Oh! Then, go right ahead!" said Captain Crook.

"Well, sir, it just entered my foul-minded brain that instead of feeding them to Janet now, ye could feed them to Janet *later*."

Captain Crook raised his eyebrow. "Why would I do that?"

"Wouldn't it be more evil to make them watch

their whole town get gobbled up and *then* get eaten themselves?" she spat on the deck.

"Ah," said Captain Crook, stroking his chin. "Dessert instead of appetizers. What a horribly wonderful idea! Spitball, you get a raise! And by that I mean you get to raise the sails on our way to New Jersey!"

Weasel ran onto the plank. He grabbed Shivers, Margo, and Albee and hauled them away. He threw them into the dark closet where he'd first found them and shouted, "Don't even think about eating any of my jams!" Then he slammed the door.

Margo leaped up and pulled on the door, but it was no use. It was locked tight.

Shivers curled up into a ball, too scared to even string a sentence together. "Monster! . . . Big teeth! . . . Gonna die! . . . AAAAAGHH!"

"Shivers, we're not going to die," said Margo.

"You mean we're going to get eaten by a sea monster and *live*?! That's even worse!"

"We're not going to get eaten. We're going to make it out of here."

"How?!"

The light bulbs in Margo's head were starting to dim. "I . . . I don't know." She leaned against the barrel of oversize fish flakes, and she slid down to the floor next to Shivers. The expression on her face fell like October leaves.

"This is all my fault."

"No, it's all *my* fault," said Shivers.

"No, it's all *both* of your faults," said Albee.

Margo put her head in her hands. "All I ever wanted was to go on adventures and sail the high seas and be brave. And look where that's gotten me. There's a sea monster about to make a salty snack out of my entire town!"

Shivers's gaze sagged to the floor. "I'm the

reason Captain Crook knows about Cheese Curd Night. I'm the one who couldn't stomach the Sea Tea. Margo, you could have stopped Captain Crook and saved your town if you had a *real* pirate for a friend. Captain Crook was right. I am just a landlubber in funny pants."

Margo looked at Shivers. She thought about all the adventures they'd shared. There were a lot of them. Four, to be exact. And none of them would have been possible without Shivers. Who better to face your fears head-on with than someone whose head is full of fears?

Margo jumped to her feet. "Shivers, forget what Captain Crook says! You might not be a normal pirate. Well, guess what? I'm not a normal kid! If you belonged in the sea where pirates belong and I belonged on the land where people belong, we wouldn't even know each other. And if there's one thing I know for sure, it's that we belong by each other's sides."

Shivers arched his eyebrow. "You mean it?"

Margo nodded. "We've only known each other for a week," she said, grabbing Shivers's hand and pulling him to his feet. "But it's been a *really* long week."

"It has, hasn't it?" Shivers cheered. "Margo, you're right. I always want to be by your side. I just wish both our sides were outside of this closet."

Margo looked around the cramped room. "Well, maybe we could feed the giant fish flakes to Albee until he's strong enough to fight the sea monster."

Shivers shook his head. "Margo, if there's one thing I learned from the year I only ate pastries, it's that flaky foods don't make you stronger."

Suddenly, they heard the bolt on the outside of the door click. The door swung open. Spitball leaped inside.

"AAAAGGH!" Shivers screamed. "She's gonna flush us *all* down the toilet!"

"Quiet!" Spitball whispered. "Did ye get the key?"

"Huh?" asked Margo.

"The key!" Spitball said, glancing nervously behind her to make sure no one was watching. "From the Bermuda Triangle!"

Shivers and Margo looked at each other, stupefied.

"How do you know about the key?" said Margo.

"Because I wrote the message in the bottle!"

"You?" said Shivers. "How did you fit your hand in there?!"

"I wrote it before I put it in the bottle!" Spitball said, exasperated. She stuck out her grimy hand. "Quick! Give me the key!"

Margo reached for the key, but then, in a flash, Captain Crook appeared in the doorway. "TRAITOR!" he snarled, grabbing Spitball and holding his sword to her throat.

Spitball looked pleadingly at Shivers and Margo. "Ye have to unlock the–"

Captain Crook clapped his crooked hand over Spitball's mouth. "That's enough out of you. And you can forget about that raise! You'll be sinking instead!"

Spitball let out a muffled cry and struggled to free herself, but it was no use. Captain Crook was too strong. He glared at Shivers and Margo. "Now you two have really gotten yourselves into a jam."

While Shivers was seized with fear, Margo seized the opportunity to escape. "Speaking of jam . . ." she said. She grabbed a jar labeled WEASEL'S JELLIED FISH off the shelf. She threw it to the ground, and it shattered at Captain Crook's feet, spraying sugary fish bits everywhere. He leaped backward in disgust. Margo grabbed Shivers's hand and Albee's bag, and then ran straight out of the closet.

"That took guts," said Albee. But nobody was listening.

Captain Crook tossed Spitball into the storage closet and slammed the door. "Get back here!" he called after Shivers and Margo.

They sprinted down the stairs, but they knew Captain Crook wouldn't be far behind. They burst into the Harpoon Saloon, where Weasel was busy mopping the floors. He still had a lot of work to do. Shiver's semidigested Sea Tea was everywhere–even on the sword-covered walls and the fishing nets that hung from the ceiling.

When Weasel saw them, he gasped. "What in the name of smoked sardines are you doing down here?!"

Margo snatched a sword from the wall and pointed it at Weasel. "Drop the mop. Or I'll slice that weird beard right off your face."

Weasel's mouth dropped open in surprise. He looked like he had been frozen in the middle of slurping up a spaghetti noodle. He let the mop slip from his grip, and it clattered to the floor.

Margo picked up the mop and tossed it to Shivers. "Now I've got my favorite weapon, and you've got yours."

Shivers gave the mop a little hug–what he called a huglet. "It feels like I'm home," he sighed.

Just then a horde of pirates sprinted down the staircase.

Shivers gulped. "Never mind. It feels like I'm on a scary ship and I'm about to get fed to a sea monster."

"There they are!" shouted the pirate with the wooden leg.

"Shivers!" Margo cried. "Get to work!"

Shivers plunged the mop into a bucket of soapy water and mopped like he'd never mopped in his entire life. Meanwhile, Margo sliced her sword from side to side, fending off the pirates as best she could. The sound of metal clanking against metal filled the air. She blocked a sword that was swinging at her head, then turned around and batted another one away from Shivers's bunny slippers. Captain Crook pushed his way through the crowd until he reached Margo and swung his sword at her. Margo swung back, sending sparks flying.

Captain Crook pointed at Margo. "Look at that, mateys! She thinks she's a pirate!" He let out a chilling cackle and raised his sword above his head.

"Okay! All clean!" Shivers announced.

As Captain Crook brought down his sword,

Margo jumped out of the way. He stumbled forward onto the soapy, wet floor. His heavy black boots slipped right out from under him, and his face smashed into the ground. As the other pirates rushed to help him, they got swept up in the suds and came tumbling down, too.

Margo sliced at the ceiling and cut down the fishing nets, wrapping the pirates up in a snarl of salty knots. The pirates angrily tried to tear themselves free, but the more they fought, the more twisted and trapped they seemed to get.

"Come on!" said Margo, leading Shivers around the pile of pirates and up the staircase.

Shivers sprinted toward the *Groundhog*, but Margo grabbed his arm. “We have to go back to Captain Crook’s quarters,” she said.

“Are you crazy?!” Shivers screeched. “We have to get out of here!”

“Shivers, if we don’t figure out what the key unlocks, all of this was for nothing!”

Shivers knew that Margo was right. They rushed back to Captain Crook’s quarters, and Margo jammed the key into the top lock on the wooden dresser. But it didn’t fit. She tried the next one. Nothing. One by one, she tried the key in all the other locks as fast as she could.

“It doesn’t work in any of them!” she said, her voice cracking with panic.

Just then, Captain Crook kicked open the door. Shivers had never seen anyone look so furious. He was sopping wet from the mop-water, there were pieces of frayed rope in his hair, and his unpatched eye was swollen from hitting the ground.

"Didn't you read the sign on the door?" he seethed. "COME IN IF YOU WANT TO DIE!"

As he lunged forward, Margo ran to the back of the room and opened the porthole. "We have to jump!"

"Margo, there's a sea monster out there!" Shivers cried.

Margo looked back at Captain Crook. "There are monsters everywhere, Shivers. Now, jump!"

That was the sound Shivers made when he collapsed on the deck of the *Groundhog*. It was also the sound that seven gallons of seawater made when it spilled out of Shivers's stomach.

Margo looked down at him and shook her head. "You really need to learn to hold your breath."

Luckily, Janet the sea monster hadn't spotted them as they made their way to the ship. Maybe she didn't have very good eyesight. She definitely didn't have very good hearing, since Shivers was screaming so loudly he sounded like a baby whale throwing a temper tantrum. It had taken all of Margo's strength to keep Shivers from sinking as she pulled him to the *Groundhog*. Albee supervised.

Shivers grabbed his stomach. "I think I swallowed a snorkel."

Margo raised the *Groundhog*'s sails and looked back at Captain Crook's ship. She narrowed her eyes at the lock on the flag. "What does the key unlock?" she said.

"I don't know," Shivers said hopelessly. "Maybe Captain Crook has a secret diary somewhere."

"Well, there's only one thing we can do now," said Margo. "We have to warn everyone at Cheese Curd Night that they're about to become sea-monster snacks!"

As the ship raced toward New Jersey, Margo found her backpack below the helm, just where she'd left it. Margo never felt right without her backpack. It was like a shield for a knight, a badge for a policeman, or an Albee for a Shivers. She took out the message in a bottle, which was now a message in a backpack, and examined it. "I can't believe Spitball wrote this."

"I know!" said Shivers, padding up the stairs to the captain's deck. "The most evil and disgusting pirate we've ever met was actually trying to help us?!"

"Turns out she's not so evil after all," said Margo.

"But she flushed Albee down the toilet! We had to scour the sewers to find him!"

"Which led us straight to the message in a bottle! Don't you see, Shivers? Spitball had to flush Albee so we would find out about Captain Crook's plan! She couldn't have told us about it while he was standing right there!"

Shivers put his hands on his hips. "So I look like someone who would jump straight into a sewer?"

"No, but you do look like someone who would do anything to save his friend."

"Wow," said Shivers, taking it all in. "She sure seemed evil to me."

Margo shrugged. "I guess things aren't always what they seem."

"You're right," Shivers said thoughtfully. "I learned that when I went to the post office. I couldn't find a single post in there!"

💀 💀 💀

Margo parked the *Groundhog* just where Shivers liked it–on the sandy shores of New Jersey Beach. By now, the last rays of sunlight had slipped past the horizon, and the moon was rising in the sky, casting a pale light across the ocean. The beach was totally deserted. Everyone in town was already getting their cheese on at the pier.

When Shivers, Margo, and Albee arrived at Cheese Curd Night, the entire pier was covered in brightly lit booths, games, and carnival rides. There were rows of stands serving up curded cheese of all kinds–fried, baked, and Albee's favorite, buttered.

"Mm, buttered cheese." Albee drooled. But nobody could tell because really, he was always surrounded by drool.

Margo stood on her tiptoes to see above the crowd. She spotted a booth up ahead where a man in a purple top hat was holding a microphone, guessing people's birthdays.

"Let's get to that microphone," she said.

They started weaving their way through the

dense crowd. Margo recognized a few of her classmates and even saw her teacher, Mrs. Beezle, chowing down on some chocolate-covered cheese curds. The Roy Scouts were there, too. They were lined up at the edge of the pier to make sure no one fell off. Shivers had never been anywhere so noisy in his entire life. Everyone was talking and laughing, and every few seconds there were shrieks of excitement from the carnival rides.

Shivers shuddered at the sight of the Tilt-A-Whirl and the Ferris wheel. "Are those designed to torture people?"

"They're rides, Shivers. They're supposed to be fun," said Margo.

"What about that?" Shivers pointed to the end of the pier, where a giant pirate-ship ride was swinging back and forth. "It's like they're trying to get seasick on purpose!"

"Some people like getting seasick," Margo explained.

Shivers held Albee's bag up to his face and shook his head. "The world is a strange place, Albee."

Margo and Shivers ran past the line of carnival games, where people were competing for oversize stuffed animals and giant neon sunglasses. There was even one game that was handing out goldfish in plastic bags as prizes. Albee was appalled.

Finally, they made it to the birthday-guessing booth.

The man tipped his purple top hat to them. "Well, hey there, kids! Do you want me to guess when you were born?"

"We need to use your microphone," said Margo.

"Sorry, this microphone is for birthday guessing only." He turned to Shivers, put his fingers on his forehead and closed his eyes. "Let me guess . . . your birthday is . . . *not* today."

Shivers gasped. "How did he know?!"

"We don't have time for this! Give us the microphone!" Margo said, grabbing the cord.

"Never!" said the top-hatted man, holding on tight. "I'm nothing without my microphone! How will people know that I have a psychic gift?!"

Margo started playing a heated game of microphone tug-of-war with the man, when suddenly she heard an all too familiar voice behind her.

"Margo! What are you doing?" Police Chief Clomps'n'Stomps barked.

Margo whirled around. "Dad! I need the microphone to warn the town about the pirate attack!"

Clomps sighed. "This again? Margo, how many times do I have to tell you? Pirates don't attack people on land."

"Captain Crook and his crew do!" said Margo, pointing at the horizon. "Look!"

Clomps turned around and saw Captain Crook's ship heading straight for the pier. Clomps's face crumpled with concern.

He grabbed the microphone from the man with the top hat. "Attention, everyone! Pirates are attacking the pier! I repeat, pirates are attacking the pier!"

Everyone in earshot burst out laughing.

"Good one, Chief! We all know pirates don't attack people on land!" said a man waiting in line for cheese.

Clomps rolled his eyes. He knew there was only one way to get these people off the pier. He sighed. "We're out of cheese curds!"

Everyone immediately stopped what they were doing.

There were shouts of "How is that possible?!" and "You'll be hearing from my lawyer!!"

In an effort to beat the traffic, the whole town

began running back toward the land. But as they neared the pier's exit, they were faced with a line of swords. Captain Crook's crew was blocking the way out. They had snuck onto the pier for a surprise attack.

Weasel was at the front of the pirate horde. He held his sword high above his head and shouted, "Hand over Shivers and Margo, and nobody gets killed!"

The pirate with the wooden leg whispered something in Weasel's ear.

Weasel cleared his throat. "Sorry . . . Hand over Shivers and Margo, then *everybody* gets killed!"

The entire pier plunged into a panic. Everyone screamed and ran around like chickens with their heads cut off–or chickens whose heads were *about* to be cut off.

Shivers's scream was the loudest of all. "AAAAAAAAAAAAAGGGGHHHHHH!"

"There he is!" said Weasel. He advanced toward Shivers, his sword shimmering in the moonlight.

But then, three oddly dressed people leaped in front of Shivers. There was a woman in pink sweats, a man in a business suit, and a teenage boy in a

Hawaiian shirt and flip-flops. Weasel's beard bristled in surprise. "Who are you?"

"I'm Tilda," said the woman in the pink sweats. "Prepare to be tormented!" Then she pulled out a giant sword.

"Mom?!" said Shivers. He looked more closely at the man in the business suit. "Dad?!" He turned to the boy in the Hawaiian shirt. "And . . . Brock?!"

"Hello, brother!" said Brock.

Sure enough, it was Shivers's entire family. They drew their swords and stepped in front of Shivers, Margo, and the people of New Jersey.

Shivers was stunned. "So your pirate mission was coming to Cheese Curd Night?!"

"That's right! We come to Cheese Curd night every year! But we never bring you along because we know it would make you *C*-sick," said Bob.

"Why are you dressed like that?" said Margo.

"So we can blend in!" said Tilda, pointing to her pink sweat suit. "We spent all day finding these disguises!"

"Even Great Uncle Marvin is here!" said Bob.

Great Uncle Marvin, the crankiest pirate in the

Eastern Seas, stuffed a spoonful of cheese curds in his mouth and mashed his gums together. "Leave me out of this!" he squawked.

Shivers noticed Uncle Marvin was wearing his usual striped pirate sweater. "Where's his disguise?"

"Right here!" Uncle Marvin said, holding up a bingo card. "They dressed me up as an old man."

Surrounded by the choppy ocean on three sides and bloodthirsty pirates on the fourth side, the people were starting to panic.

"What are we going to do?!" cried a man from the crowd.

"We're surrounded by danger!" a woman screamed.

"I should have stayed home and fried my own cheese!" called someone from the back.

Tilda turned to Margo and Shivers. "Margo, as the bravest person here, you need to get the people to safety. Shivers, you go with her. We'll fend off the crew."

"But Mom!" said Shivers. "These are the roughest, toughest pirates in the Seven Seas!"

Bob took one look at Weasel and sneered. "Pirate Code breakers? They're not real pirates; they're just a bunch of sealubbers in funny pants."

"I bet they talk back to whales, too!" Brock shouted. "Let's get 'em!"

As Shivers's family set to work fighting back the pirates, Margo led the people to safety. She had to gather everybody in one place, somewhere she knew she could protect them. She climbed onto the pirate-ship ride. "Everybody on board!" she commanded.

"You want us to get on a pirate ship? That's terrifying!" someone from the crowd said skeptically.

"I thought the same thing," said Shivers, "But believe me, pirate ships are much less scary when Margo's the captain."

"Now move it!" Margo added.

She was so commanding that the townspeople didn't care that she was only a fifth grader. She was clearly braver than the whole bunch put together. They made their way onto the pirate ship.

Meanwhile, Bob and Tilda rushed over to the row of cheese-curd stands. They pelted the pirate crew with gobs of mozzarella and launched marinara sauce into their good eyes. Some of the

pirates managed to get past the cheesy deluge, but Brock and Police Chief Clomps'n'Stomps were waiting for them. They grabbed the code-breaking pirates by their tattered vests and threw them onto the Ferris wheel.

Marvin sat at the control panel. As soon as the pirates were loaded in, he pulled the lever and sent the Ferris wheel spinning at super speed.

"Buckle up, and don't enjoy the ride!" he said through a mouthful of cheese curds.

It looked like Shivers's family was getting the upper hand–or upper hook–on Captain Crook's crew. But then Janet the sea monster rose up from the water and let out an ear-scraping screech. She opened her giant jaws and took a big bite out of the middle of the pier. The whole town screamed in terror as the cheese-curd stands and carnival games tumbled

into the sea. The bright, colorful lights that lined the pier bobbed below the surface, casting an eerie glow in the water.

Captain Crook had arrived. His ship floated next to the pier. He stepped out onto the deck and, with a smile as wide as the horizon, bellowed,

"SAY CHEESE!"

CHAPTER FOURTEEN

"TAKE COVER!" MARGO COMMANDED as the whole town backed into the corner of the pirate-ship ride and stared in horror at Janet.

Shivers held Albee's bag up to his face. "Albee, what are we going to do? Blink if everything's going to be okay."

"I'm a fish," said Albee. "I don't have any eyelids."

"WE'RE DOOMED!" Shivers screamed.

Janet took another enormous bite of the pier, sending more carnival games and fried food into the ocean. Captain Crook laughed at the destruction. But when he saw his pirate crew trapped in the spinning Ferris wheel, his expression turned from delight to disgust.

Weasel was stuck at the very top of the ride. He rattled the bars and cried, "Captain Crook! Help!"

"You make me sick!" Captain Crook frowned. "'Send us ahead for a sneak attack,' you said. 'We'll take all their money and cheese,' you said. Some evil pirate horde you are! Beaten by a bunch of landlubbers!"

"We're not landlubbers; we're pirates!" Brock said, brandishing his sword.

Captain Crook looked back and forth in confusion. "Then where are all the landlubbers?"

"They're over there on that pirate ship!" shouted Weasel.

Captain Crook scowled. "What's going on here?! Pirates on land? Landlubbers on ships?" He started pacing back and forth. "You know what? Forget it. There's only one true pirate in all the Seven Seas. Me!" He leaned over the edge of the deck and shouted, "Janet! Eat them all!"

Janet bared her sharp teeth, then crunched through another huge piece of the pier–this time even closer to the pirate-ship ride.

Margo had to think fast. She couldn't just let her whole town sit there like snacks waiting to be swallowed. If only she had been on a real pirate ship, she could have sailed them to safety. That's when she got an idea. She leaned over the side of the ship and pulled the lever, starting the ride.

"Margo! What are you doing?!" Shivers cried, as the ship swung back and forth.

"Trust me! Just hold on tight!" she shouted.

Margo raced to the front of the ship and climbed up the beam that connected the ride to the pier. Every time the ship swung up, everyone screamed because they were so high in the air. Every time the ship swung down, everyone screamed again because they were right next to the sea monster. Really, it was nonstop screaming.

As Margo reached the top of the beam, she saw the Roy Scouts below her. They were passing out pamphlets on how to stay safe inside a sea monster's stomach. Roy strummed his guitar and sang "The Sea Monster Mash."

"Roy!" Margo held up her hand. "Spork me!"

"Aye, aye, Captain!" said Roy. He tossed his pocket spork straight up, and Margo caught it. She reached up and pried off the heavy bolts that connected the ship to the pier.

Captain Crook's voice cut through the chaos. "Eat them!"

Just as Janet snapped her teeth at the swaying ship, it sailed off its hinges into the air and landed with a splash in the sea. The whole town shrieked so loudly that Shivers finally felt like he had something in common with them. The end of the pier crumbled into the water, along with the last of the carnival games.

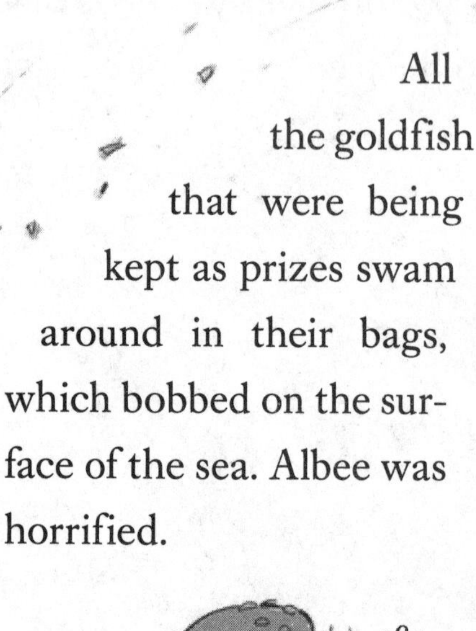

All the goldfish that were being kept as prizes swam around in their bags, which bobbed on the surface of the sea. Albee was horrified.

Captain Crook turned to Shivers and Margo. "You can run, but you can't hide!" he shouted. He sailed toward them, and Janet followed alongside.

Margo slid back down the beam to the front of the ship, but there was still no way to steer. As much as it looked like a pirate ship, it was really just a giant hunk of plastic with a couple of skulls painted on the side.

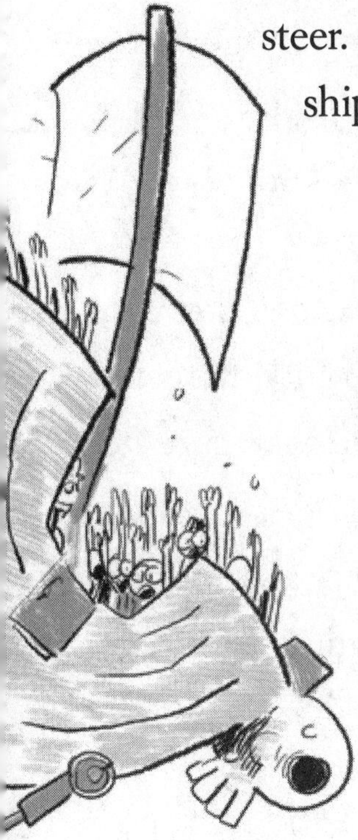

"Well, this is it," said Margo. "As the captain, I have to go down with the ship."

"Wow, Margo, you really are the bravest pirate I've ever met," said Shivers.

She smiled at him. "I learned from the best."

They turned to Albee. "Albee, you supervised."

Albee was staring down at the goldfish in the ocean, trapped in their plastic bags. "Actually," said Albee. "I'm done supervising!" And with that, he puffed up to his full blowfish size, tearing open his bag, and leaped into the water below.

Shivers and Margo watched in awe as Albee swam through the choppy waves, using his blowfish spikes to pop all the bags and free the goldfish.

Shivers marveled at Albee–his mouth closed tightly, his body puffed up with air. "So *that's* how you hold your breath!"

Janet was catching up fast. As she sped through the water, Shivers spotted a glint of shiny metal near her tail. He looked closer to make sure he wasn't seeing things. Sure enough, something was wrapped around her back flipper. And then it dawned on him–which was strange because it was the middle of the night.

The key to stopping Captain Crook.

He turned to Margo. "Give me the key!"

Margo's eyes flickered with concern, but she handed him the key from her backpack. "What are you doing?"

"I'm doing exactly what you taught me. I'm facing my fears head-on."

Captain Crook screamed with all his might, "For the last time, eat them!"

Janet opened her mouth wide, and Shivers dove headfirst into the ocean. He hit the icy water and held his breath as tightly as his lungs would allow. He plunged deeper and deeper, forcing his eyes open through the sting of the saltwater. Then he saw it . . . a rusted chain wrapped tightly around Janet's flipper, binding her to the side of Captain Crook's ship. The chain was secured with a big metal lock. Shivers

was running out of air, or rather, swimming out of air. He had to act fast. His best friend, his family, his first mate, his whole town were counting on him. He stretched out his arm and put the key in the lock. It fit perfectly. He turned the key, and the lock snapped open.

Shivers kicked his way to the surface and gasped for air. Albee swam up next to him. Everyone on the boat was shouting at Shivers to get out of the water. His family stood at the broken edge of the pier, more terrified than they'd ever been in their entire lives.

"Shivers! Albee! Swim!" Margo urged. "That evil monster is going to eat you!"

Shivers flapped his arms to keep himself afloat. "She's not an evil monster! She's just a big fish that got caught by an evil pirate!" He turned to Janet. "You're free now, girl."

Janet blinked her beady eyes at him and slapped her fins against the water happily.

Captain Crook grabbed the railing of his ship and stared down at Janet, his face red with fury. "Listen to me, or I'll chain you to the bottom of the ocean!" He pointed at Shivers. "EAT THAT PIRATE!"

Janet opened her massive mouth and bared her razor-sharp teeth. As she brought her head down, Shivers let out one final squeak. But she didn't eat him. She plucked a piece of seaweed off the side of the ship, slurped it up, and smiled . . . as much as a sea monster can smile.

"Awwww!" Shivers squealed. "She's an herbivore!"

Then Janet swung around, lifted her long neck, and ate Captain Crook in one big bite, swallowing him whole.

"Never mind," Shivers corrected. "She's an omnivore."

CHAPTER FIFTEEN

"ONE, TWO, THREE, PULL!" Margo shouted.

It was the next morning, and for the second day in a row, Shivers's ship was connected by a mossy rope to Captain Crook's old ship. Which was now Spitball's new ship. Well, slightly used ship.

The *Groundhog* lurched forward. It was still stuck in the sand, just how Shivers liked it, but it was edging closer to the sea. As soon as the first tiny wave splashed the tip of the ship's hull, Shivers called out, "Three, two, one, STOP!"

Now, the *Groundhog* had found its new home. It was perched halfway in the water and halfway out.

"Thanks for your help!" Margo unhooked the rope and tossed it back to Spitball.

"It be my salty pleasure!" Spitball replied. "Anything I can do to repay ye for rescuing me from the Cap'n."

After Janet had slurped up Captain Crook, Shivers and Margo had freed Spitball from the storage closet.

Spitball continued, "I thought I'd be livin' out my days on Weasel's dried salmon skin and stale sea slugs."

Shivers shuddered. "Gross."

"Hey, I heard that!" said Weasel from over by the mast as he lowered the flag with the iron lock and raised a flag with a glistening glob of spit.

Some of Captain Crook's crew had joined Spitball on the ship, vowing to always follow the Pirate Code under her leadership. Others chose to stay on land and become bankers, teachers, and popcorn-ball makers. As the crew helped remodel Spitball's new ship, they hauled out

Captain Crook's locked chest of drawers and prepared to toss it overboard.

"Wait a minute," Margo said. She still had one question that hadn't been answered. "If the key from the Bermuda Triangle didn't unlock any of those drawers, what was Captain Crook keeping in there that was so secret?"

"Clean socks!" said Spitball.

Shivers, Margo, and Albee were stunned. "Huh?" they said at the same time.

"The keys he kept around his neck unlocked all his precious sock drawers," Spitball explained. "If yer ship is full of bloodthirsty, untrustworthy pirates, ye have to lock up yer valuables. Clean socks are hard to come by when yer drifting about in the Great Blue."

"That's why I love my bunny slippers," said Shivers. "No socks required."

Shivers and Margo watched Spitball reach into the barrel of extra-extra-large fish flakes. "Janet!" she called. "Snack time!"

Janet the sea monster's head popped out of the water. Spitball tossed her a giant fish flake. Janet chomped it up in one bite. No longer chained to anything, she swam around in the waves, happy and free as could be.

"If you think that tastes good, try fish flakes with butter!" Albee called to Janet.

Margo and Shivers waved good-bye to Spitball and her crew as she sailed into the Eastern Seas.

Just then, Shivers's family climbed aboard the *Groundhog*, along with Police Chief Clomps'n'Stomps. They were all eating ice cream.

"Shivers, you were right!

Ice cream is delicious! I'm so glad we finally get to try it!" said Tilda.

"And we don't have to disguise ourselves anymore!" Bob added. He and Tilda were back in their fearsome pirate clothes, which the sunburned sunbathers on the beach no longer found so fearsome.

Brock was still in his Hawaiian shirt. "I'm never taking this off," he said. "I sailed all the way to Hawaii to get it!"

"You know they sell those in New Jersey," said Clomps'n'Stomps.

Brock scratched his head. "I thought they only sold jerseys in New Jersey."

Shivers walked over to Great Uncle Marvin. "Why are you still covered in cheese curds?"

"That's not cheese curds; that's my skin!" Marvin spat, then took a big lick from his raisin-flavored ice cream.

Margo and Shivers laughed. They walked to the ship's railing, Shivers carrying Albee in his fishbowl. They looked to the beach, and then to the ocean. People and pirates didn't seem so different anymore.

"Well, Shivers, we did it," said Margo. "We saved our town."

Shivers smiled. "And I think it's even better than before."

As they stood half on land and half in the sea, they knew that they could belong in both places at once. And for the first time ever, Shivers wasn't afraid of anything at all.

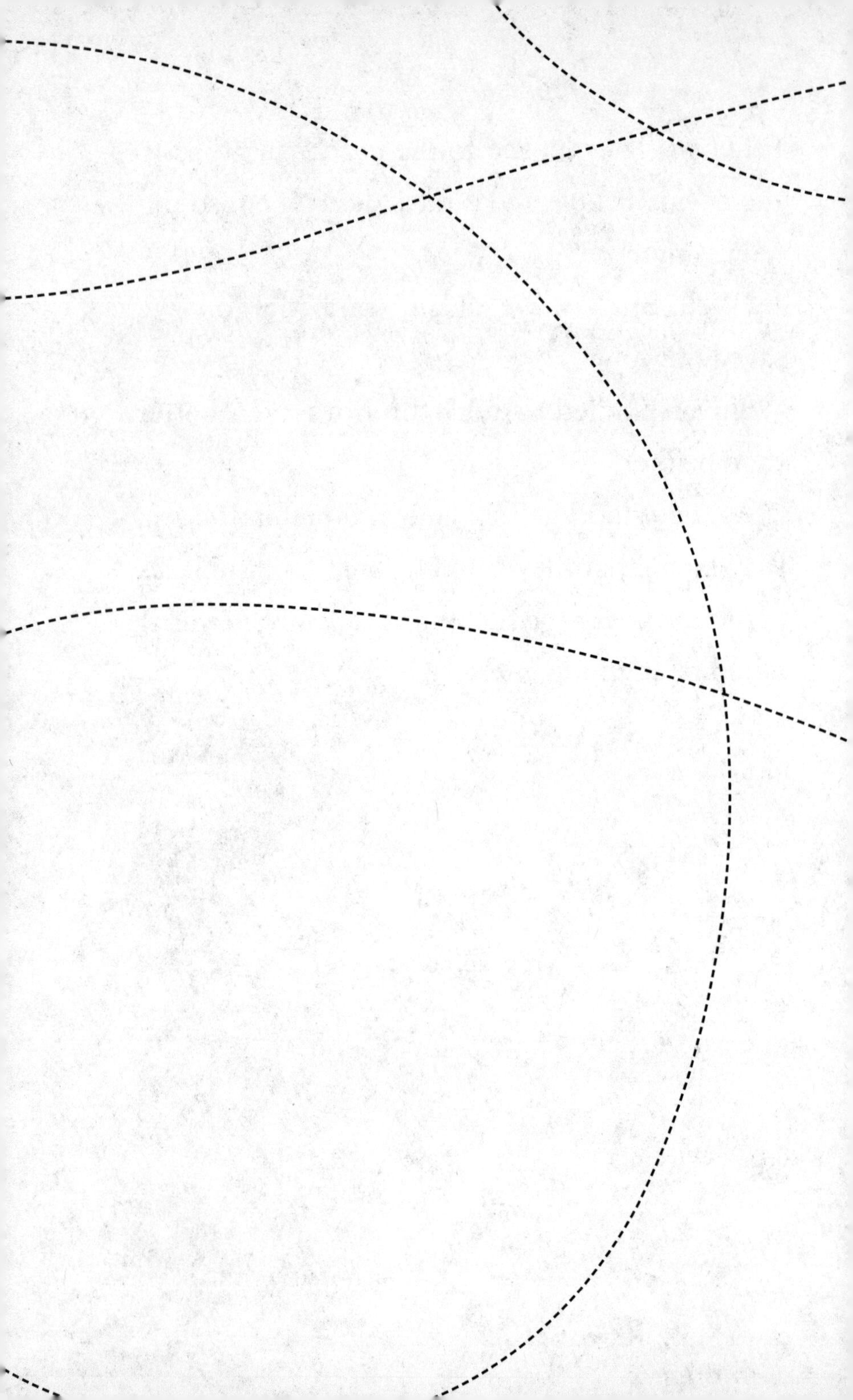

THE END!

OR IS IT?

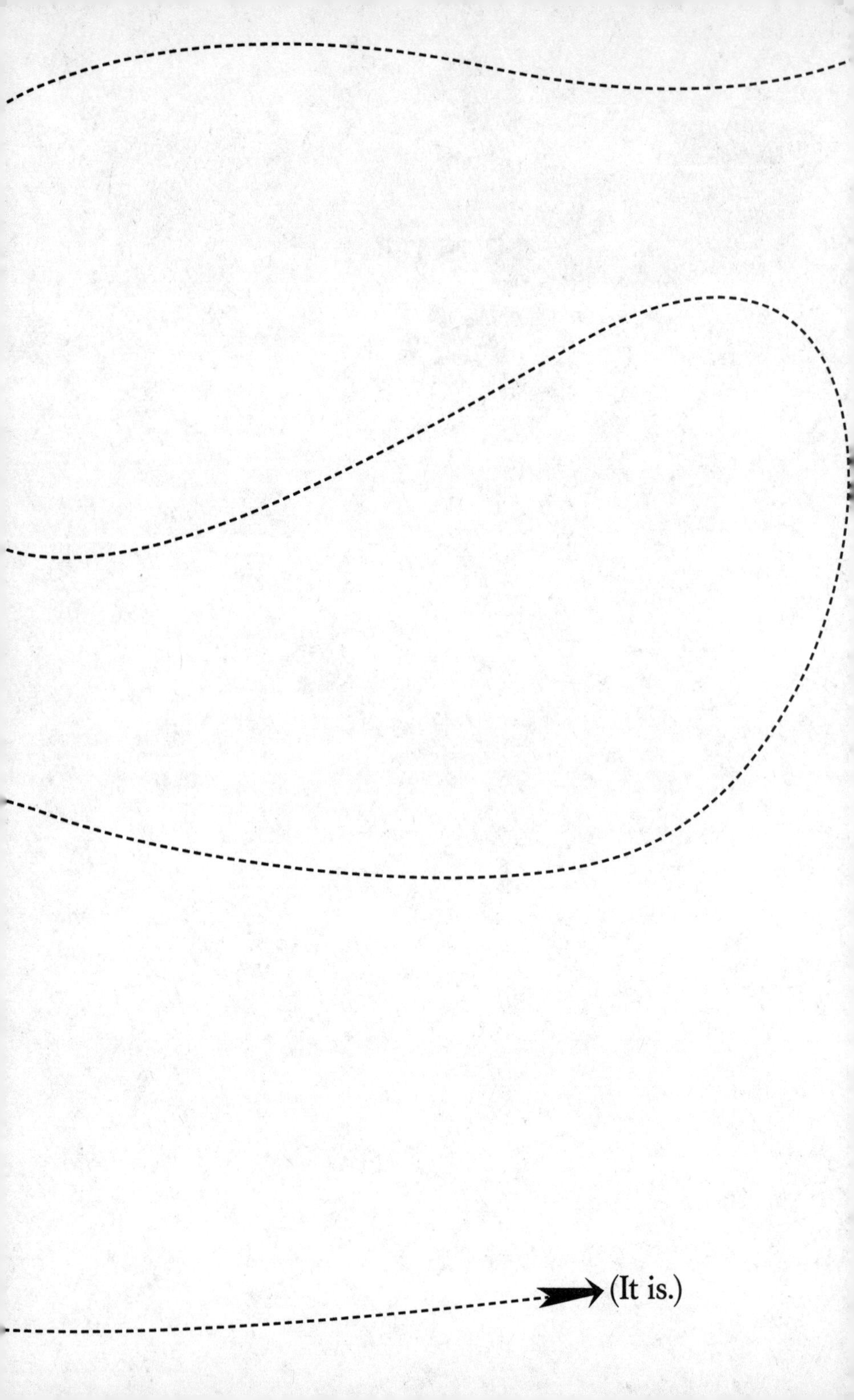
(It is.)

Annabeth Bondor-Stone and **Connor White** are also the authors of *Time Tracers: The Stolen Summers* and *Jaclyn Hyde*. Their work has been translated into multiple languages and featured on the Chicago Public Library's Best Fiction for Young Readers list, as well as the Huffington Post.

After graduating from Northwestern University in 2009, Annabeth and Connor moved to New York to eat huge slices of pizza, then moved to Los Angeles when they got full. Now they travel to schools across the country using comedy to inspire kids to read and write. You can follow them on Twitter @ABandConnor or follow them around in person if you live in LA. Find out more at annabethandconnor.com.